RENT BOY

AND OTHER RELATED STORIES

DAVID WISE

Rent Boy And other related stories by David Wise

ISBN 978-1-952027-08-6 (Paperback)
ISBN 978-1-952027-09-3 (Hardback)

This book is written to provide information and motivation to readers. Its purpose is not to render any type of psychological, legal, or professional advice of any kind. The content is the sole opinion and expression of the author, and not necessarily that of the publisher.

Printed in the United States of America.

New Leaf Media, LLC
175 S. 3rd Street, Suite 200
Columbus, OH 43215
www.thenewleafmedia.com

CONTENTS

CHAPTER 1

THE FIRST

The lay preacher placed his hand upon my shoulder and guided me over to the table. As I stood there he placed a two shillings piece down on the table and moved away not saying anything. I knew at once the significance of the coin and I stood and stared at it not knowing what to do.

When I was very young around five or six I was reckoned to be old enough to play out and joined the local boy gang being the youngest of around seven or eight boys. As the youngest I became the butt of their jokes and was often punched or hit and tripped as the lowest in the pecking order. After a few weeks I got used to the punishment and liked all the attention. One time while we were playing at the local sewage works we climbed onto the filtering tanks. These tanks were about six feet deep of stones set in a circle. At the centre was a pipe where four large pipes spread out in the form of a cross about six to eight inches above the stones. Water poured from the pipes and drained down through the stones being filtered. The gang made me strip and lay down to let the sewage water give me a bath as it passed over me. It got bad some weeks but I looked forward to being punished and to see what they would do to me. One day we were down on the canal tow path where a couple of barges were moored with the mooring rope stretched across the tow path made from crushed cinders, and tied onto an iron ring fastened into the canal bank. As we passed by someone pushed me over and I tripped over the rope and fell heavily throwing out my arms to guard my face. Both arms hit the cindered path and I felt great pain as the cinders tore into my flesh. I had to be taken to the hospital to be treated and left with both arms bandaged where the damage was. This time I didn't enjoy the pain. Two day's later mum gave me and my brothers a treat by allowing us to go to the pictures. I was seven years old and in those days we used to roam all around the town and countryside without anybody worrying about being safe. We settled into our seats and watched the film until it ended and I wanted to go to the loo. The gent's lavatory was full and I waited until most of the men had gone and then tried to undo the buttons on my trousers. They were a bit tight and the bandages were stopping me bending my fingers to release them when a voice enquired if I was having trouble and would I like some help? I'd heard that some men interfered with boys and that I should be very careful so I said yes and allowed him to fiddle with my pants and handle my little Willie. He was very gentle and I thanked him when I'd finished after which he gave me a nice smile and left. I returned to my seat to enjoy the film and didn't see him again although the danger bug had aroused in me and the next time I was in the cinema I purposely sat by any shifty looking men that I could find. It took a couple of visits but this one gent appeared very interested and as soon as I was seated his arm was on the armrest dividing the two seats. Soon after his hand draped itself over the arm rest and down onto my side of the seat touching my leg just under my shorts and then stopped. This wasn't what I wanted and so I took his hand and gave it a little squeeze. He glance at me and smiled turning back to look at the screen but his hand now stroked my leg going up under the shorts. When I didn't object he moved over to the belt buckle of my shorts and deftly unclipped the snake fastening and the top button allowing him access to my body. Soon he was caressing nearly all of me under my shirt and finally down inside my trousers. Shortly afterwards the film ended and I said that I would have to go and maybe we would meet again sometime. He smiled and nodded but didn't try to follow as I left the cinema. I had a few more of such encounters at the cinema but that was as far as it went and even the old gang now seemed as though they didn't want me around.

The year drew to a close and Christmas neared. At school our teacher decided to have an essay or as he said we had to write down a story of what we would like for Christmas. What were are ambitions for Christmas. All the kids around me were going to write about meeting Santa Claus or seeing an Angel or getting a fabulous present or a holiday and such usual things but I decide on something completely different, something the teacher wouldn't want me to put down in my exercise book. I turned to the middle pages and eased the top two pages from the wire clip for I knew he would want to remove it from my schoolwork and then I wrote; I want to be a Rent Boy. I want someone to take me and pay me for using me for his sexual pleasure. He would take me and I would stand still and be stripped and put into bondage to make sure that I couldn't change my mind, and then give me a spanking to prove who the boss is. After that it would be up to him as to what he would force me to do. The payment will be two shillings and if paid will be for my silence as to what he does or who he is. I finished the paper and placed it back in my book and handed it in at the end of the lesson. I expected to be called to the Headmaster's office as soon as we returned to school after Christmas. When we did return my teacher didn't mention the story and I wasn't asked to read it out or give any explanation or receive a summons to the office nor any punishment. It was just as though the story had been forgotten. For Christmas I received a small train set consisting of a circle of track and a little tin train with two coaches. When wound up the train used to go off at such a pace that it threw itself off the track and if not fully wound would not pull the coaches at all.

Christmas passed and was just another memory. The little train had been discarded as being useless so it meant one more holiday when I didn't get any presents but I knew that we couldn't afford presents as my dad was already working all the hours he could at his low paid work, so much that we hardly saw him at home. It was January and school work carried on as normal. I was looking forward to my eighth birthday just a few weeks away.

Sunday morning came around and we had to attend Sunday school at a church a little way from where we lived. The adults held there own service in the main church and the children used a little school across a small playground where we were taught by helpers until the main services were over and parents collected their children on their way out. Everybody left the school and I had put on my coat ready to go home as my parents didn't attend church as dad worked and mother had too much to do. As I walked across the playground the Lay preacher called out to me to come into the vicar's manse. The vicar was away at the time and the preacher was staying in the manse and taking the services. I entered the little hallway and was shown into a kitchen. When there he stood me besides a table and then fumbled in his pocket and brought out a two shilling piece which was placed before me. I was wondering what he was doing when he'd guided me to the table but when he'd placed the coin down then suddenly I remembered the essay. Surely he didn't know about that I thought, but he didn't say anything as he waited to see if I would pick up the coin. Well this is what I asked for I thought as I put out my hand and fingered the coin and then picked it up and put it into my pocket. The preacher didn't say a word but strode over and picked me up placing me onto a chair. His fingers unfastened the buttons of my coat and slipped it off and even at this time I was still wondering if I should call a halt and run out from the manse, but that old feeling of wanting to be ill used suddenly kicked in and so I stood perfectly still not moving or saying anything. My little sleeveless pullover followed and then my one good shirt leaving me naked above the waist. He walked around to my rear and I felt the pull as he took my arms and pulled them around my back and fastened both wrists with tape. I realised that I was helpless and it gave me a little shock to think that now I was his prisoner and he could do whatever he wanted to do. My shoes and socks were pulled off without the laces being untied. My pants soon followed and my ankles tied. I was now naked and in bondage as he picked up the clothes, placing them into a cupboard and then sat on the chair with me kneeling between his legs where he proceeded to fondle me all over. I was laid across his knees with my head hanging down when suddenly his belt cracked onto my naked bum with such a force that it made me yelp with pain. This wasn't the usual spanking but full blooded blows. I tried to lift my legs to protect myself but he held the tape binding my ankles and blows kept coming until I started to cry. He stopped seemingly satisfied with his work and then carried me up to a bedroom where he laid me on the bed. I could hear a bath being run and after a while he came back into the bedroom and I saw that he had undressed and didn't use a towel. It was the first time that I had seen a naked man as he lifted me from the bed and took me to the bath where he lifted me into the water. It was hot and soapy as he got in and pushed me down to a kneeling position and then used a big sponge to soap firstly me and then himself. My hair was shampooed and the hot water poured over me. This was the first time that I'd ever used shampoo or a big sponge and proper soap as at home we had to share the bath as we couldn't heat up any water except from the back boiler at the downstairs fire and that took two hours and a great deal of expense, money we didn't have. After drying I was back on the bed at least clean and warm. He came to the bed and once more fondled me started to kiss me on the lips and told me to open my mouth and lick his tongue. I later learned that this was a French kiss. He wanted his whole body kissing and licking pushing me further down until I reached his genitals where he opened my mouth and pushed his penis in and made me lick and suck it until it grew large. After a while he gave a soft moan and discharged a liquid into my mouth and then made me spit out the liquid onto a saucer. A few minutes later he arose and left the bedroom.

I was taken back into the bathroom shortly afterwards and saw that he had redressed. He told me to swill out my mouth and then he released me taking me back downstairs to my clothes. I felt the two shillings as I made my way home. Except for the last little bit the experience wasn't too bad. When I arrived my mum pounced on me and demanded to know what I'd been doing. She could smell the shampoo and the soap and knew that something was wrong. I told her what had happened and she told me to stay there while she went to see the preacher. When arriving back I was asked about the essay and told her about the two shillings. She told me that if anyone else asked me to go with them then I had to see her first. It appeared that mum had made an arrangement with the preacher for more money and the next Sunday the preacher was waiting for me. When I'd been stripped and beaten I mentioned that I didn't need beating every time but he said that it was a sin and that the beating was my punishment although he didn't mention what his punishment was.

I realised that if the preacher like to beat me then others may like to also, especially if I did anything wrong or failed to please them in any way, and that could mean being hurt. I decided that what I needed was training but who do you go to for that kind of training?

My dad was reading his newspaper and on the rear was a report of a youth who had been fined for interfering with young boys, and he lived very near to our house although I didn't know him. With his name I checked all the addresses in the area through the local council voting list and found his address and with this I wrote a letter to him. I'm eight years old and will be sitting on the second bench from the local park gates on a Friday night. If you are interested come between 6pm and 7pm and then it was posted that night.

It was a fine night and quite warm. The wait could be boring and so I'd brought a comic to read while I waited. Nothing happened for a while but I didn't worry as he was probably checking to see if it was a trap and maybe some of the men had decided to teach him a lesson and give him a beating. When he could see that the area was clear he would make his move if he was interested in meeting me. The park clock struck seven and I waited for ten more minutes but nothing happened and so I decided to go home. As I stepped through the park gates and onto the pavement a voice suddenly spoke to me from the far side of the gate pillar. "Did you write this note," said a voice. I turn around and a youth was holding my letter. Nodding I asked him to go somewhere to have a chat. We went back into the park to a bench half hidden by the trees and sat down.

"I want learn how to be a rent boy but I'm not sure of how to be one and what they should know, and what to do and how to do it to please a man. If you teach me I'll come to you and let you strip me and place me in bondage so you can do what you like to me and make me serve you whether I like to do what you tell me or not. I'll want paying for my service the sum of two pounds. By giving me this money that'll make me a rent boy offering sex for money and that means I can never tell anyone about what we do. Are you interested in teaching me?" The youth thought about it for a moment and then nodded his agreement but said that he could only afford five shillings and so I agreed as I wanted to be trained.

"Good, the best time for me would be on the Saturday afternoon but we don't want to be seen and so you have to find away to get me into your house."

"I usually take my laundry to the shop on the Saturday; can you fit into a suitcase?"

"If it's not for too long, I don't want to suffocate." I replied.

The next Saturday we arranged for me to be at a small car park at the top end of the park at one pm. At the appointed time an old blue ford pulled up and with nobody around I strolled over.

"It's my dad's," said the youth, but he can't drive. "It was left over from the war and going very cheap so I drive him where he wants and keep it for the rest of the time". The boot was large and so was the suitcase. We set of as I climbed into the case and around three or four minutes later we arrived. The youth opened the boot lid and glance around before reaching for the case lid.

"I'm just going to close the lid for a couple of minutes just in case someone sees me taking it out of the car." All went dark and the lock clicked shut. Hope he's got the key I thought as I was thrown onto my back as he picked up the case and carried it into the house. The next few weeks I became his play thing as he instructed me in what men wanted and then made me carry out his instructions. The main instruction was that skin is just skin and if you are kissing someone than no matter where you are kissing it's just skin and nothing more, and you wouldn't hesitate if you were kissing a hand or someone

one on their cheek so anywhere else its all in the mind. I went to him each week until I felt that I wasn't learning anything new and he was simply using me for his own pleasure. I knew then that it was time to go.

One Saturday the usherette at the theatre started to talk to me as I waited for the film to finish on the afternoon performance and then start again for the evening show. The cinemas did three shows per day. She had obviously seen something as men would sit besides me and try to fondle me. I told her that it was alright as I was a rent boy and was picking up clients. She seemed surprised but if any men entered the auditorium and looked about looking for young boys she would seat the man near me. She also let me use the dearer seats as they got a better class of men.

One day the friendly usherette showed a gent over to where I was sitting and he sat down next to me. I could smell his scent or aftershave he was using. Nobody that I knew used scent and the smell seemed overpowering to me. Soon his hand was straying over the armrest of my seat and to show him that it was alright I give it a little squeeze of encouragement which had become my usual way of showing that I was available. The gent appeared a little embarrassed that I knew that he was doing and so I took his hand and placed it on my knee. The man seemed relieved and relaxed by placing his arm around my back and gently pulling me towards him. I whispered that perhaps he would like to move a couple of rows towards the rear as there were some double seats that courting couples used in the last show. Soon we were in the seats where there wasn't any arm rest between us. The usherette passed bye and I gave her a quick smile as my gent started to loosen my clothing and exploring my body.

The film ended and the news adverts, and a second feature started that neither of us wanted to see and so he suggested that we left the theatre.

"Would you like a ride in my car? " He asked and pointed to a large car parked along the street. Cars were very few and far between and I had very little chance of having a ride so I gave my best sweet smile and nodded. The car was an Austin and the top of the Austin range with a big engine and leather seats. We drove to the outskirts of the town and pulled up outside a large house and sounded the horn. After a few moments we were joined by another man who climbed into the driving seat. My gent put me in the rear seats and then sat beside me as we set off to a little lay-by about two miles out of the town. After parking I was pulled onto my gents knees and then slowly undressed. Shortly afterwards the men swopped over and the driver climbed into the rear seat beside me and pulled me onto his knee.

When both men had finished I was redressed and we set off back to town. Arriving after a few minutes my gent took out his wallet and gave me £2 and then asked if I would meet them again. I decided to be a bit cheeky and said that I would if they would take me home. I told them that if they parked a little way from my home then I would see the car and knew to meet them later. That evening I walked into our house and placed the two pounds on the table. As dad earned about £6 pounds a week labouring they were amazed that I had earned so much in a couple of hours. From then on my gent became my best client.

The vicar arrived back from his holiday and that put an end to the hot baths and we had to use the wash basin in the small school but it wasn't the same and I missed the hot water and good smelling soap and shampoo.

A week passed, the preacher asked me to ask my mum to come and see him after the Sunday school children had left. When she arrived they talked together for a while and told me to wait as I was going with the preacher to another house. I wanted to go home and play out for the rest of the day but I didn't get any choice. I had to stay in the washroom of the school as all the other children left and all the congregation of the church had gone home and the vicar retired to the manse. The preacher had a small car that was a familiar sight around the area. When I got in I had to crouch down in the well of the passenger seat with a rug thrown over me to hide me from view. We rode for about ten minutes and pulled up in a driveway of a house where I was to get out and walk around to the rear where we were let into a kitchen where a man was waiting. The preacher talked for a moment and then left leaving me with the stranger who led me upstairs to a bedroom where he took great pleasure in removing my clothing. Now I knew what my mum was discussing back at the school and knew that she must have agreed a price for me to come to this new man. The new man tied my arms and ankles and gave me a spanking. Later when we were having a bath and I told him that there wasn't the need to belt me and he said that he was told that I liked to be spanked. Clearly he had seen or been told about the school essay.

Two months had gone by and my men had now risen to six when mum was asked to see a man whom we all knew and he had a bad reputation as a hard man that you do well to stay clear of especially if you wanted to borrow money as some of our friends did. As far as I knew there were only the banks that loaned cash and if you were poor then you couldn't get a loan. At the weekend mum took me to where this man lived and there a car was waiting for us. We set off at around five in the evening going over into Lancashire to one of the mill towns, stopping just on the outskirts at a large mansion type house. We were kept downstairs in what would have been the servant's quarters and given sandwiches and tea and told to wait. More children came until there were four boys and three girls all around my age waiting in the kitchen. Around 8.30 – 9.00 we could here car engines and the slamming of doors as guests arrived for a party. Music sounded from the stairs and then a man came and said they were ready. All the children including myself were then stripped and the man led us up the stairs to the bottom of a large staircase where a number was tied around our necks, and then we had to line up with the boys on one side and the girls on the other. Two of girls were sobbing but nobody came to wipe away the tears as guests wandered past with ladies going up the stairs to a powder room and the gents to a smoking room just off the hallway. After a half hour or so a boy name Dave who was wearing the number three was called by a man standing at the top of the stairs. He was taken up to a long corridor with several doors and told to stand outside a door where the man gave a small knock and the door opened and Dave was pushed in. Dave was by far the prettiest of all the boys.

He had long blond locks of hair and deep blue eyes and a baby face so it was no surprise that he would be the first to go up stairs as we all by now had guessed why we were there. By eleven pm I had been up the stairs twice and most of the other had also had trips up with Dave getting most of the attention. Suddenly it was over when we were led away as a group of older girls took our places. These girls were around fifteen or sixteen and were scantily dressed. They immediately started to flirt with the men who passed near the stairs. I watched for a minute until our group was led away. Downstairs were more sandwiches and hot drinks and once fed and back in our clothes the man from our town had a word with my mum and the night was over. The car was waiting to take us back home. The man who had arranged for me and the other children to be at the house was there organising the events. It was he who controlled all the girls and seemed to have a hand in all the activities going on, he was the kingpin, the man in charge. I had started being a rent boy on my own but wondered just how many of the other children and girls had been forced to do his bidding.

CHAPTER 2

PHOTOGRAPHS

"We're going over to Lancashire on Saturday so don't get lost". Mum said to me on the Friday night. That meant to stay close to the house so she could call me in when it was time to get ready to go. I pulled a face as I didn't like going there and didn't like the man who had asked, but knew that it was all arranged without asking me if I wanted to go. Saturday came and a shout told me it was time to get ready. I dressed in my school clothes as it didn't matter what I wore as I wouldn't be wearing much when we arrived. The car was waiting for us and we set off. The car was a small one and had little power as it climbed the long road over the Pennines. At that time there wasn't any motorways and the journey could take a long time. After what seemed an age we finally arrived at eight. A man told mum that we were on at nine but nobody explained just what he meant by that. The place was the same mill complex as the previous one but this time we parked in the mill yard and not the large house. Tea and sandwiches were provided and then we waited on a row of chairs. The basement was quiet and it appeared that all the other kids had either finished or gone home or that I was the only one but then a man entered and told me to get ready which meant to get undressed. The man took my hand leading the way to the lift and up to the attic. We entered and I saw a group of men talking and drinking at a makeshift bar set up in one corner. A circle of chairs were in the centre of the room and a footstool had been placed in the middle of the chairs. At the side of the chairs was a film camera on a tripod. It looked just the same as you sometimes see in old movies but had an electric lead. The men seemed not to be in a hurry as they smoked and drank giving me time to study them. All were well dressed in expensive suits and all wore gold pocket watches with Albert's attached to gold chains. After twenty minutes a small bell sounded and gradually the men finished their drinks and wandered over to the chairs. The man holding me pulled me around and tied my arms behind my back.

I wasn't concerned as this was often done to me. A strong light lit the circle as the person who had been holding me appeared but this time he was holding a small camera. He once more took my hand and I was led to the circle and given to one of the men sitting on the chair. The sound of the camera sounded just behind my ear as the man sitting ran his fingers all over me and then passed me over to the next man and so on until I had been all round the circle. After the filming I heard the film being change and also the large film unit came close. The little bell sounded again in walked two young men of about thirteen to fourteen. The clack, clack, clack from the cameras as both were in action echoed throughout the attic filming the boys. Both wore short white overall coats but when the reached the circle they dropped them and stood naked for all to see. Shortly they both walked over to the men and stood in front of them allowing their bodies to be felt and groped as they moved around the circle. The cameras followed but were kept pointing a bit low and not filming the men's faces. I was wondering what was going on when the small bell tinkled again and I was pushed onto the footstool lying across it with my head over the other side. The boys came to me with one going behind me and the other kneeling at the front. A jar was placed on the floor beside me with a short stick like a piece of broom handle. The boy behind me unscrewed the lid and dipped in the stick. The filming carried on with the camera now coming very close and not missing any of the action. The other boy placed his hands on my shoulder pressing me hard down and suddenly a pain like I've never felt before brought a yelp from my lips as the boy shoved the end of the stick up my backside and proceeded to twist and turn it only pulling it out to replenish whatever was on the stick and inserting it again. The pain was unbelievable and I tried to move but was held still. I felt the stick pulling out and thought that it was over but I was wrong. Something else was being inserted and I realised that I was being raped. At this point the boy in front pulled down on my ears and forced his penis into my mouth ordering me to suck it. I was being ill-used at both ends and there was nothing that I could do about it. The gathering of men were shouting encouragement to the boys but they didn't need any as firstly the one behind and then the one in front reach their climax and withdrew. They stood to take the plaudits from the group of men as a collection was started. Both film cameras ceased filming and their operators compared the shots they had taken. The strong lighting was turned off and the room returned to normal lights. I was lifted up and taken back down the lift with the tears still running down my face only to face an inquest from my mum who thought that it was just a filming session and nothing had been said about being in a rape scene. No money was shared from the collection and no drink was offered to me as we were told that the car was waiting to take us back home. On the road back home mum questioned the driver and found out that our local man had known about the rape scene and had been paid extra money that should have been passed over to us but clearly hadn't been. Mum decided enough was enough and we would have nothing more to do with our local man but to tell the driver to ask his boss to contact her directly if the wanted any more filming but no rape scenes. The local man controlled the telephone near to where he lived and from where all the instructions came but he had his girls outside the phone box waiting for calls and anybody wanting to use the phone would get threatened. Mum managed to arrange a go between to pass on our calls.

The next week there were some new toys in the house and mum got her first new little washing machine, a twin tub called a wash dog.

Two more filming sessions following the rape session but this time we knew exactly what the film wanted and what we'd agreed to. The money doubled from what we were getting before and as mum said it just showed how much the local man was creaming off when paying us before. We only saw the man once but he didn't speak to us and we ignored him.

On the second occasion we were there, my mate Dave from the first session was also present. While we were waiting he told me a story of what he did in the summer holiday. This is Dave's story.

One day at the very end of the war a couple's little girl caught one of those child diseases that was going round. These diseases killed lots of children in infancy and there weren't any antibiotics in those days to cure them and you just had to take your chance. Things like diphtheria, scarlet fever, mumps, consumption and many more could and did strike at any time. The couples little girl caught one of the diseases and it proved fatal. The little girl was four years old and had blond hair and blue eyes and when they were taking a walk in the local park Dave's mother was there taking a walk with him. The lady started to cry as Dave was the spitting image of her lost baby girl. They got to talking about the sad occasion and their sudden tragic loss. At the end of their talk Dave's mother agreed to visit. During the visit the lady showed the room belonging to their girl, a room packed with clothes and toys but only one photograph. The lady said that they didn't have any photos because they couldn't get hold of any film for their camera in war time. The picture was just as though someone had taken a snap of Dave and put it in the picture frame, the images could have been twins. Between the two ladies they decide to dress Dave in one of the lost little girl's dresses and take some more pictures as nobody would be able to tell the difference. The following week Dave was posed in the dress and looked beautiful. The tried more of the dresses and took more pictures and soon the snaps were back from the shop after being developed and placed around the room in picture frames. The visits grew into weekly visits until Dave's mother grew ill and had to go into hospital for a small operation. Dave's mum was war widow and had nobody to care for Dave. It was suggested that Dave stayed with the lady because she would love have a toddler around the house as she missed her lost daughter so, although Dave was a little older. On the day Dave's mother had to go into hospital Dave was left with the lady. First thing to do was to give him a bath and new clean clothes which were of course one of the dresses from the lost girl's bedroom, and not only the dress but all the under garments too. When finished dressing him the lady had her little girl back with her again.

Dave's mum was ill and in the hospital for almost three months and Dave used to visit every week. When released from the hospital she needed a period of rest and recuperation and so Dave stayed with his new mum. The lady and her husband loved having Dave around and living with them. His name was changed to Rosemary which was the name of the little girl that they had lost, and he had his own room in a large house and plenty of toys and pets to play with. Everything was fine until the day finally came when it was time for Rosemary to go to school. Rosemary couldn't go as a little girl and so had to return to his real mum and become Dave once more.

Dave's mum lived on a small pension in a rented little house and things were very hard for her as frequent bouts or illness meant that she couldn't work but Dave looked cute and she was asked if he could be used for some photographic work and this helped to pay the bills but life was always a struggle for her. One day she was asked if gentleman could borrow Dave for an hour but just for a little petting and nothing too serious. Two large bills for electric and gas had just come in and so she agreed. Soon Dave had a string of clients and had become a Rent Boy.

Every year he used to return to his second mum and become her little girl Rosemary during the annual holidays where they used to go on holiday for two weeks and then spend the next two weeks at home. Then it was back to school as Dave. Time passed and Dave's mum got worse and could hardly manage around the house. There was talk of her having to move into a home and that would mean Dave too would have to move into a children's home. The Lady was upset at losing Rosemary as it would be like losing a second child and then her husband came up with an idea. If Dave's mum would allow it they would adopt Dave as their son and also allow his mum to move into a little cottage in their grounds where she could live free of worry and see Dave most of the time. They would provide him with private education and he would lack nothing and hopefully be taken in to the family business if he wanted. Dave's mum agreed that it would be best for Dave and after the adoption Dave would move and start his new school after the summer holidays. I was glad for Dave but I realised that it would mean the end as a rent boy and that I wouldn't be seeing him again.

That night was a night of posing for the camera while they did some still shots. It involved a lot of being chained up and pretend rape and the usual carry on that I'd come to expect but there wasn't any rape or pain it was all pretend. When we'd finished and back downstairs one of the film directors came to see us. I was asked if I'd like to do some filming on location in a church. Transport would be laid on and a bed for mum and me would be provided as the filming was at a church and late at night. The money would be about three times what I normally got. The church was paid for their building to be used to film the scenes but not what the scenes were. I believe they thought it was to photograph the church from the inside to show the beautiful carvings and so it was but along side the film for the church would be the one being made by me.

One Saturday night the car arrived. This was a big limousine just as the film stars used. There were sandwiches and drinks in the car as we were going straight to the church arriving around seven pm. The film crew were already setting up their equipment and the area had been roped off for safety reasons. I recognise the men doing the filming as the same men who filmed when I was raped and hoped that they would keep their word. The next hour was for a rehearsal or as it turned out several rehearsals. The scene was for me to beg for attention from the vicar but he had no time for because he was taking a service. I therefore stripped and waited in the little pulpit and when it was time to deliver his sermon he would find me there. He couldn't do anything as I was without clothes and couldn't be removed, and so he had no choice but to carry on. As he started I then had to creep with my hands up his legs under the cassock and then pull down his pants and taking them off. The problem was his facial expression that he couldn't get just right. One camera was on his face and another was on me rubbing his underpants while he was trying to carry on with the sermon. Finally off came the underpants and then I rolled up his cassock showing him naked from his waist down as I licked his bum. There were six rehearsals before we got it right and then I think that it was because it was growing late that the scene was finally shot.

"That's a take," called the director. He must have thought he was in Hollywood instead of shooting a sordid sex film, but as long as it paid well I should care. The car drove us to a hotel where we could spend the night and the following morning it brought us back home. The next day mum opened a bank account for me the first in our family to have one. I had to meet her in town during lunch time as it was a school day, and then sign my name in a little book that said I'd got fifty pounds credit. This was huge sum for a boy to have and more than most adults had to their names.

During the next two months we only did one more photographic session. When I was dressed and ready to go mum and I were approached by one of the men. He asked if I would like to take part in some torture sessions. He explained that some people had a fixation about torture and not only liked to watch it being done on other people but like to take part. They volunteered to be tortured. They had a safe word given to them and then the person doing the torture had to try and get them to say the word. There were five levels with the first one involving being whipped. During the whipping the victim was stripped and hung up by his wrists. If he didn't give in a heavier whip was used. It progressed until a cat o' nine tails was the final one but nearly all men would have given in long before then.

Some of these sessions could go on for a long time with some of the extreme victims spending their holiday being tortured. These were usually more of the endurance type torture. They would be stripped and put into small cages and fed on bread and water for days. They could be chained and beaten and blindfolded for hours. If they used their safe word they were released but having paid they would lose their money. Some would like a film of themselves being tortured and it would be even better if the torture could be done by a child, that's where I came in. I was asked if I would like to take part at the weekends when the film cameras were there. Sometimes the torture could go wrong and someone would overstep the mark and get carried away when trying to get the safe word from a victim and would seriously hurt him. Several of the men there wore scars from whips or cuts and bruises but I never heard of any very serious injuries apart from one.

I thought about it and talked it over with my mum but although I liked an occasional spanking this was going a step too far and so I declined. I never saw anyone get any serious injury from the torture room but I was told of a story that could be true or was It just a leg pull. You can decide when you read it.

Two dairy farming brothers were both into the torture scene and used to attend sessions together. They ran a small herd of cows and would bring in a bull to breed from. They raised a few calves and had their milk to make a good living. A few fields to raise crops gave them the extra income to take an occasional break. The only other person on the farm was a man who looked after the cows and fed and milked them and he knew what to do and just got on with the work. The milking parlour was a little way from the farmhouse because of the smell. A wagon would call for the full milk churns and leave the empty ones, and every thing worked like clockwork.

One day the brothers were together in the calf shed. They had a fine crop of cows that year and also six bullocks. The bullocks were of no use for breeding as they didn't have a great pedigree to sell on and they couldn't be use on their farm in case of inbreeding, but they could be used as beef cattle either to keep for fattening on selling on to another farmer for fattening in case they were a bit short of cash. Either way the calves' needed to be castrated to calm them down. The castrating was usually done about a week after the calves' were born and by that time they could be quite large and heavy and a kick from a hoof could be painful and so they were moved from their shed to the next shed where a special pen would hold them. The pen was three sided and narrow. The calf was let in at the rear and then couldn't turn around. At the front was a hole where the head passed through and then was clamped so that the calf was restrained in the device until the deed was done. The farmer or vet uses a burdizzo to crush the blood supply or a less painful method putting on a small rubber ring by means of an elasticator that stretches the ring at four points and then it is release once in position over the scrotum thus cutting off the blood supply. The two brothers didn't use a vet as the procedure was a simple one of using the rubber band method with the elasticator. The bands were made from a hard rubber and once in place wouldn't shift until weeks later they would drop off and therefore needed no cutting. The first calf was let into the pen and soon was let out with deed done. As they were getting through all six one of the brothers suddenly said he wondered what it was like having the band put on, to which his brother said to try it and see. After a bit of banter he said that he would try it. They decided that a good test would be for about a day and then cut it off. It was agreed that the first brother would be the calf and would strip and be penned in the device and have the band fitted and then remain in the device to stop him from changing his mind. His brother prepared the elasticator with another band.

Having stripped the brother was led around to the opening and walked on all fours sticking his head through the hole. His brother then placed a chain around his neck tightly fastening it to each side, and walked around to the rear and picked up the elasticator. Moments later the first brother gave a sharp yelp as the elasticator was released and the band closed around his scrotum. He was asked how it felt and was told it was like someone was squeezing the life out of his balls.

The calves' were taken back to their shed and just then the milk wagon arrived and he went down to lend a hand with the loading. The churns were left on a little platform at the same height as the wagon's loading back. The brother stepped onto the back, skidded and fell falling over the side and hitting his head on the road. When they got to him blood was pouring out of a wound and so an ambulance was called for. It was half an hour before they got him to the hospital and found that he had a fracture of his skull and was unconscious. Two day's later he became aware again but didn't remember what happened. His farmhand called in for a visit on the afternoon of the third day to say that all was fine and the work was going on and he was looking after the calves, and when would his brother be back. It was only after that the man had gone that he remembered where his brother was and had someone released him. The nurses wouldn't allow him to get out of bed and so he asked for the telephone to be brought to him. As they were busy it was not until the evening that he heard the trolley being wheeled into the ward. He decided to ring his old doctor who had recently retired from active practice but was still a good friend of theirs. He told of his accident and that he was still in hospital and then told of what took place earlier that morning and said his brother may be still trapped in the device. The doctor wasn't told about the elasticator.

It was about 11am before the doctor arrived at the farm but the farmhand said the other brother was away and he didn't know when he would be back. The next day he visited the hospital to report what he'd learned only to be told the truth and that the brother was trapped in the calf restraint device and had been for five days. The doctor now drove to the farm as fast as he could and asked where the calves were castrated. When he got there he found the brother slumped on his knees still inside the device. He freed the man and took him to the house to get some fluid into him. After looking at the rubber band he thought it best to leave it alone as there was a lot of swelling and it would have to be cut off but it was too late to save his testicles as they had turned black through a lack of blood. Nature would have to take its course and in time they would drop off just like the calves and the band would also fall off.

Two weeks later both men had recovered and had resumed their work on the farm and nobody knew about what had happened except the doctor who let it slip to one of his friends at a party but didn't say who they were.

That's the story believe it or not. It is hearsay but then again who is to say that it's not true.

HARRY

Harry was around my age and the last of the boy's that I used to see on a regular basis going to the various houses that were used for parties. Some boys I'd see now and again but I always could count on Harry to be there and have someone to talk to as we waited to be selected to do our duty.

His mother was a single mum who liked a wild time and would be at any and every party that was going at the time. At that time there wasn't the drug scene as there is at today's parties and that was probably because there wasn't the money around to make it worthwhile and it wasn't until the late fifties that the first drugs entered the scene and they were LSD and not cocaine and Heroin but there was the main drug, alcohol. The parties that Harry's mum liked were the ones that provided free booze and she would get her fill and if it had to be bought then she would pick up a willing feller who would keep her supplied for a quick trip to her home. It was at one of these trips that she ended up a little too worse for wear and her partner for the night was a little upset and started to get angry and said that if she couldn't do it then he'd take the boy. She thought that was funny and started to laugh before falling to sleep still half dressed. When she awoke it was to find the boy on the floor naked with tears stains on his face telling a tale of a man pulling him from his bed and doing terrible things to him.

Two weeks later she was as usual trailing the town looking for a free party but to no avail. Having no money and nothing in the home to eat she was looking for a man to take her to the pub and ran across the same man from a couple of weeks ago, the man who had taken her son. He knew that she was desperate for a drink and offered to take out but as an appetizer wanted to have the boy first. Free booze for the night or the boy for fifteen minutes, it was no contest and Harry had a new occupation as a rent boy.

Harry slept for most of the day and seldom went to school. Whenever the local authority started to ask any questions then they would move to another district or town and the paper work would get shelved and lost. One day word came that I was wanted for a party. At this time pubs and clubs closed at 10pm but if you knew where to go then a drink could be had. Every town had pubs where a private party was going on and even the police had their places to go to after they had finished their duty for the day. This party was a special very private one and in a secret location, the torture room. I was to report at 7 pm in town where I met Dave and Harry and some of the staff I'd seen on my nights doing my duty. We were all loaded into a large van and driven around for a while before stopping at either a mill basement or a farmyard barn. Once inside the place was blacked out but well lit inside as steps led down to the torture room. At the sides were the cages and each one held a naked man who was handcuffed and had a black bag placed over his head. I was also told that they were gagged to prevent any speaking. At the other end was a drinks bar and in the middle a dance floor. It would be our task to carry the drinks for the guest and of course we were to be naked.

I needed to go to the lavatory before we started and found two of the cages were in place for the guests to pee on the victims inside. What a laugh the guests would think. I just shook my head in astonishment.

The band arrived and started playing as the vans brought the guests with the men making for the bar and the woman having a laugh at the naked men in the cages. From then on we were busy carrying drinks as the dancing started and went on until 2 am when the vans collected the dancers and everything fell quiet. The band had a drink as we dressed and we travelled with them back home.

Harry took the job in the torture room but his mother drank all the money that he made. She died in her early thirties of liver disease.

Extreme rent boys are in the torture category. They take the greatest risks and therefore receive the greatest money. One that comes to mind was a boy called Raymond or Ray for short. Ray lived with a mate in a small flat in London back in the 1950s. His flat mate was called Derek and he too was a torture rent boy. Both Ray and Derek were only fourteen years old and both had run away from a children's home somewhere in the north and had been found living on the street by their mentor who had found them a small flat and introduced them to working in the sex industry. One summer when the rent was due the couple had just come back from their holidays and were a bit short of cash. Their mentor had a job for them for some middle easterners. Nearly all of the boys had a mentor to look after them and run them to jobs for a percentage of the takings, and they were no different as a job meant money and so they took the job. Derek was taken to a flat in the east of the city and Ray was at one in the centre.

The task of the rent boys was to please their masters but in the case of an extreme rent boy it meant to do anything the master required usually spread over the weekend. They would report or be taken to the place where they would be working and once there it was not unusual to be grabbed and stripped naked and be given a beating with a belt if they didn't do as they were told as most of the men who took part in these sessions were unfeeling brutes who liked to torture their boys. The boys were often as not then tied up or chained up and forced to perform sex acts on or with their masters with once more the threat of the belt if they didn't please the master. Throughout the day they were made to serve the master until he'd had enough and then they could rest for a while. Sometimes they were forced to wear costumes or dresses and then act as waitresses all day before being stripped once more and taken to bed and having to perform more sex acts throughout the night or when required. The next day it would start again or they were tied and used as a foot stool until the master had recovered. To be a torture rent boy was risky and could be painful but it did pay well. An average wage would be around £10 per week for a working man but a boy could earn around £50 for a weekend and if he really pleased his master he could get a bonus on the top of his fee and that could mean a lot of money for a boy.

A job came in for a boy and they asked if Ray was available. It was unusual to ask for a boy by name as they didn't give any names but in this case they appeared to know about him. As it was for the middle easterners Ray said that he'd do it. His mentor told him that it would be on a boat but wasn't told where the boat was moored. Ray was to be taken to a place where a car would take him to the boat. That arrangement meant that the mentor didn't know where they were taking Ray to and he would be on his own. Ray said that he would still do it and was told to be ready on the Friday.

On the appointed day and time Ray's mentor arrived and they set off to a meeting place where another car was waiting. A man who appeared to be of Arab appearance greeted them in perfect English. He told Ray to strip and leave his clothes with the mentor. He undressed down to his white underwear that he was allowed to keep and the man gave him a medical examination and when he was satisfied allowed Ray to get into the car and that was the last that anybody ever saw of Raymond. When he didn't return at the set time the mentor made enquiries of the easterners he usually dealt with but they denied that they had ordered any date with Ray and they didn't know who had. The mentor put the word out that Ray was missing but nothing was heard and it seemed that he had disappeared from London but where to? All his things in the flat were never touched and none of his friends were contacted, and as he'd no relatives he was reported as a missing person to the police but in the capital lots of kids would run away from home. I think that someone had seen Ray when he was working on a job and took a fancy to him. The reason to meet way out in the countryside was twofold. One not to be seen and the other to be near a small airfield or grass strip where a small plane could land. They were probably right when they said that he would be on a boat but where was the boat? I think that it was somewhere on the continent and that Ray is now someone's real life slave boy serving a master who's home is in the Middle East But that's only my guess. Derek was heartbroken at Ray's disappearance and begged his mentor not to forget him but to try and find out where he'd been taken to. His mentor tried but was unsuccessful and all his enquiries fell onto deaf ears. After three months Derek was convinced that Ray wouldn't come back and he too decided to leave and it is believed that he went back to the children's home from where they both had absconded.

CHAPTER 3

RALPH

Ralph loved dogs, big or small, smooth or hairy, brown, black or white any kind of dog at all. Once a month I had a regular date with him to go to his house but not to be used for sexual purposes but to simply play ball and I don't mean to cooperate but to throw a ball and let him chase it as a dog would, well it takes all kinds. Ralph is a farmer or was a farmer because he no longer farms after an accident damaged his back. His farm is for the present leased out to a neighbour while he recovers and if he can't get well enough it will then be time to decide if it will be sold.

The farm house is fairly modern with four double bedrooms and a garage with some outbuildings surrounded by fields. Ralph lives in the house as the farmer who at present is leasing the farm has his own place on his own farm and so Ralph is isolated and not bothered by anyone which is just as well as it would looked very odd if anybody was strolling past to see a naked man running after a ball. I forgot to mention that he didn't wear clothing as not only did he like dogs but that he wanted be one. He would get down on all fours and wait patently as I removed his clothing and put a collar and chain around his neck and then lead him to a small paddock at the rear of the house. He reckoned that being on all fours and running around helped to ease any pain from his back and so I would throw the ball and watch him bounding after it to retrieve it. Sometimes we would play Pointer. This is where I would throw the ball but he wouldn't watch where it lands and then I would guide him to it by means of hand signals as a shooter would to a retriever and then when he'd finds it he would stand still and point at it with his nose waiting until I give him the signal to bring it back to me. I didn't see how this could help his back but maybe it just helped to relax him as after a brisk workout of ball chasing a large grin would appear on his face as though he'd really enjoyed the session. The only drawback to these workouts was for me as it was a bus ride away from my home and took time to get there and have a session and then take the bus back. Normally my men would pick me up in their cars and drop me off again.

One day in late July when I was getting ready to return home after our usual workout Ralph said that he wanted me to do him a favour. He asked that the something special he wanted to do would mean coming to see him at least every other day. This request was of the greatest importance to me as every other day at that time of the year would mean that I couldn't go on my holidays. I was going to give him a flat refusal when I paused; I wanted to know what was the special something that he wanted to do? Ralph told me that he wanted to experience what a dog would experience in real life in a farmhouse being out on its own all the day tied to a kennel and only seeing someone maybe once a day when they were fed. I was going to say pretty bored when it suddenly struck me that he was going to ask me to do the same to him. I thought that this was a daft idea and told him so and he'd either die from hunger or freeze to death from exposure, but he simply laughed. I then asked what he would be eating as in 1948/9 there wasn't tinned food that you could just wander into a shop and purchase as nearly everything was hand served and wrapped. His reply was that he'd eat the same food as any other dog or do without, and anyway he could do with losing a pound or two. That posed another question as to what I would be paid as it would interfere with my holiday and any other of my clients who wanted to book me, but to every question he had an answer and so after overcoming my objections I agreed. I was to put him into his collar and chain and call to feed him every two days and not let him free no matter what he says or does or how he pleads that he's had enough.

Ralph had a housekeeper who called in twice weekly to do a little cleaning and generally make sure that Ralph was alright. He said that she would be given the time off as he would tell her that he was going on a visit to some relatives in the South and he'd not be back for a month. That only left the farmer to whom he'd leased the land who might get suspicious if he saw me coming every other day but he thought that a casual mention to him that I would be calling would allay any question of whether I was up to no good. Next he showed me the spot where all this was going to happen. At the rear of the small paddock where we played ball was a small fence. We strode over and walked to a copse of trees standing on a hill and being surrounded by the fields without any pathway leading to it. The farmer didn't use the copse and had no reason to go into the trees. Just in front of the trees were some bushes that hid the base of the copse and when we approach I saw a kennel at the side of a tree. Ralph took me to the kennel and I saw that a chain had been placed around the base of the nearest tree and led to the kennel. Just behind a small latrine had been dug and a feeding bowl was waiting to be filled. The kennel was just large enough for a big dog but not a man. The only way that Ralph could enter was to curl up without any room to stretch his feet out. There wasn't a door and so it was open to the elements for all of the time. I kindly pointed out that if it rained then there wasn't any shelter for him and being cold and wet wasn't a good idea but he simply said that dogs have to put up with it but I replied that most dogs have thick coats to protect themselves, and anyway he'd soon break the kennel and find a stone to break the chain and be back indoors. He gave me a wink and said that he wouldn't be able as he'd thought of that. My next question concerned the dog food and where would I be able to purchase some and what kind of food would it be? Ralph said that the food would have to be horse meat as this was the only meat going and everything else was rationed. The shop where the meat was sold also sold bones but I don't think Ralph would be able to chew his way through a big horse bone. Some dog biscuits were available but these were very hard but Ralph said to buy them and break them up with a hammer and sprinkle onto the meat. Everything was settled and he wanted to start on the following Monday. I was given a small purse of money and told to report at ten to help prepare him, but he didn't explain how or what to do to prepare for his ordeal.

Monday morning I trailed into town to the place where the butchers shop was located and queued up with the rest of the crowd. When my turn came I asked for the meat only to be questioned as to why I wanted it as some people used it for stew if they were short of money, but I told him that I was looking after a big dog for a month. This appeared to satisfy him and I carried my purchase to the grocers where I bought a pound of dog biscuits. The wicker shopping basket was heavy as I waited for the bus and I thought that I could detect a strong smell just starting to ooze out of the wrapping paper but then the bus came and I rushed upstairs to be away from the other passengers. Fifteen minutes later I walked up the little lane and headed for the house. Ralph was waiting for me and asked if there was any trouble getting the meat. I told of the butchers suspicions as to my intention in buying the meat and Ralph grinned and said that he wasn't far wrong. He showed me how to cut up the chunks of meat into a dish and then add water and bring to the boil to soften it. I thought that this was cheating as the dogs wouldn't be able to cook theirs but he said that it was only a little bit so he thought that it was alright. We broke the biscuits and sprinkled some over the meat and then we were ready.

Ralph brought a large bowl and poured a quantity of powder into it and mixed it with a spoon. Next he brought two gloves of black rubber and put them on. Now with his help I removed his clothes and he produced two more gloves covered in fur which were slightly larger than the black rubber gloves. He pulled these on and got down on all fours and told me to pour the mixture into the large gloves. I lifted the bowl and started pouring and as I did he moved his hands to make sure the mixture seeped into every corner of the gloves. When he was satisfied he stood very still until it set hard. A hook at the top of the glove attached to a tape was taken around the wrist and hooked onto a clip and secured the glove. I had then to put on his hind feet and fill those with the remaining mixture. A large bushy tail was strapped on and his chain and leather collar fastened and he was ready. A quick look around showed that all was clear and we set out to the copse. It was a little awkward for him with his hands set rigidly in the gloves that prevented him from bending his wrists and having to climb the fence but we managed and soon we were hidden by the trees. At the side of the kennel I pick up the chain and locked it onto the collar, he was now helpless to remove it. I dropped the bowl of food and wished him luck, told him that I would see him I two days and left. I could see his wistful gaze as I disappeared into the trees and wondered if he was thinking just what has he done but it was too late now as I wouldn't be back for two days. Tuesday it rained all of the day and into the early hours of Wednesday morning but then cleared into a nice sunny day.

At around nine I went into town to the butchers shop and bought some more horse meat. As I had plenty of biscuits I could catch the bus in town and save myself a walk. I dropped off at the little lane and started up to the house when suddenly a figure was approaching. I just saw a woman's hat bobbin towards me through the leaves of a bush and quickly jumped into the bushes and lay down. The woman was the housekeeper who had been given the time off and even so her usual day was Tuesday not Wednesday. How was I going to be able to cook the meat with her on the prowl and what explanation could I give if she suddenly walked in. I couldn't say that I'm here cooking horse meat for Ralph who's chained to a kennel in the wood, and what about the smell from the cooking meat? If she returned she must be able to smell that as it filled the whole kitchen. I decided to consult with Ralph before I did any cooking.

When I reached the copse I paused before entering just to make sure that nobody was around and the housekeeper hadn't returned. No one was about and so I dashed into the trees and called out that it was me. I found Ralph curled up in his kennel looking forlorn and shivering from the cold and wet. He clearly wasn't well and told me that he'd made a mistake by having sited the kennel with the opening facing the prevailing wind and had been drenched for two days by the rain. With him clearly suffering and having the housekeeper around it made it impossible to go on. He agreed and said he will try again in two weeks. I unclipped his collar and helped him back to the farmhouse. Once there I took the hammer and gently tapped the gloves to break the plaster. Soon he was free and went upstairs to take a hot shower while I got rid and the debris. When he returned he was a new man saying that he must turn the kennel around and his dog food required a little salt to help it go down. One hour ago he was chained naked in a kennel and dying from exposure and now he was planning a second attempt. We were interrupted by the sound of the front door being opened. He motioned to me to go out of the back door and to see him again in one week. With that I picked up the meat and made my getaway.

The end of July was showery with a steady wind however the forecast said that there were some good weather coming for a few days and so Ralph decided to have another try at the beginning of August. On the Saturday I once more set off to the butchers for some meat on a fine warm morning.

With plenty of biscuits left from the first attempt I took the bus to the little lane and up to the house. The first task was to turn the kennel which we did only to find that it was now facing the little latrine trench which wouldn't be good. Ralph searched around for another suitable spot but there wasn't anywhere where the kennel was hidden from view and he thought that the farmer would want to know why a kennel had suddenly appeared in the middle of the copse and come looking only to find him naked and chained. We turned the kennel back to its former position and return to the house. Ralph went off into his workshop and returned with a piece of canvas and a hammer and nails. We once again returned to the kennel and nailed the canvas so that it could be pulled over the doorway in case of rain. He seemed satisfied at this solution and decided to proceed. In the house I started to mix the plaster as he brought out the gloves and paws along with the dog tail. Soon I was pouring the last of the plaster into the rear paws and fastening on his tail and we were ready. The pan of dog food that I had put on the gas stove was bubbling away and the biscuits were ready and waiting to be sprinkled over the top. In a half hour I should be on my way back home.

At the kennel I clipped on his chain and left his food but couldn't help noticing that if it rained or the wind blew, the piece of canvas would be blown about and would soon tear itself free but Ralph was settling in to his kennel and curling up before going to sleep. I decided it was time for me to go. I said I'd see him in two days and left.

The weather was warm and dry and when I visited on the Monday Ralph was in fine form and said he was enjoying being a dog listening to the birds and watching all the wild life. I gave him his food and watched as he ate it. I filled his drinking bowl and seeing that everything was alright decided to leave. On the Wednesday once again everything was alright as the weather held good but that night the forecast said storms were going to sweep in and a strong wind was expected. The storm struck on the Thursday evening and was ferocious with high winds and rain lashing down. I began to worry about Ralph and his bit of canvas and would it hold up to the storm. Instead of going to town for his meat I decided to go straight to the Kennel. I had an uneasy feeling as the rain hadn't eased and now there was hail to make things worse. The little lane was almost impassable with large puddles and pieces of bushes that had been blown down. The farmhouse looked alright but as I set off across the little paddock the appearance of the copse didn't look the same. When I arrived I couldn't see Ralph. The kennel looked good and the piece of canvas was still in place although being blown about but no Ralph. Behind the kennel was a large branch that had fallen from one of the trees. By following the dog chain I saw that it disappeared beneath the fallen log. For one moment I thought that Ralph was under the tree but as I rounded the branch I saw him laid out alongside where the branch had dropped onto the chain when he was out of the kennel at the latrine trench and he'd been unable to move the log from the chain and had been forced to spend the night chained in the open in the middle of a storm and worse was that it was a hail storm. He was almost unconscious from hypothermia as I unclipped the chain and as before tried to get him to the house. Ralph was so bad that he couldn't walk and I had to drag him most of the way until we arrived at the paddock with its fence where I knew he couldn't get over and so I had to try to get him under the lower bar. Ralph was murmuring something as we finally reached the kitchen. I ran a bath of hot water and almost carried him up the stairs not bothering to take off his paws full of plaster but I did manage the tail and his collar and got him lowered into the water. I left him to warm up and went to make a mug of coffee. On returning I was glad to see that his eyes were open and he was able to take the mug from me using the two paws. "Thought I was a goner that time," He took another sip of the coffee.

"When the branch fell and missed me I thought that I'd got away with it but then realised that the chain was underneath it and that I was trapped. Too heavy to move, the only thing that I could do was to wait for you and by the look of it just in time or I'd be up in dog heaven."

After an hour he was able to put on a dressing gown and descend into the kitchen where I could get busy with the hammer to get the paws off his hands. I opened a can of soup for him and saw him tuck in as I carried the bits of plaster to the outside bin. When he had finish he pushed the dish away and said "I think I'll give up being a dog. They're lovely creatures but after two close shaves I think someone's trying to tell me something, so I will thank you for your services but don't think I need them any longer." For once I agreed with him. I've lost clients before but this time I wasn't sorry to lose him although he was one of the nicest men I've ever know. I walked down the lane clutching a good bonus and knowing that I didn't have to walk back.

CHAPTER 4

An Adventure

Doug was ten years old and an orphan. He had spent all his life in an orphanage and knew nothing else. More than ever he wanted to travel to other countries and see new places, do new things and have different experiences but it was obvious that he wasn't going to get the chance stuck in the home. On the wall in his tiny room were pictures of famous cities from around the world and above all was a picture of the Empire State Building that he'd like to visit but there was no hope of going there. At the home the only break the children had were occasional day trips away to the coast or the zoo and sometimes to a local farm to see how food was produced.

One day in the early spring the children were out on one of these trips where they would be taken on a trip to a ferry which would take a sail around the harbour and back in time for tea and the coach home. Just in front of their ferry was another ship a little larger than the one they were taking and this ship was going to France. As they were waiting to board, a large group of children filed past heading to the larger ship. As the first group passed Doug noticed that one of the tickets tied to the lapels of the children's coats had fallen off. Doug quickly picked it up, tied it to his coat and as the second group passed he tagged along at the rear. The official at the other ship was checking the tickets and seeing that all was in order waved them aboard, Doug was off to France. He watched as his original ferry cast off for its trip around the harbour and back as his ship started on its way to France. What he would do when he arrived he didn't know but it was an adventure and a chance to see somewhere different.

The ship docked in France at Calais and all the children disembarked to go sightseeing around the town. Doug joined them and then wondered what to do next. He could just return on the ferry and go back to the home but he wanted more and having got this far he didn't want to go back just yet. It was possible that the people from the home had found out that he was missing and may be searching for him and it wouldn't be long before the others in his group would tell he'd boarded the wrong boat. He had to get away from Calais as soon as he could. A map in the town showed an arrow pointing to the south and it was as good as any direction so he started to walk. He left the town and on a long stretch of road came across a small group of trees where a little lay-by had been built and there was a car where two people having a drink. The car had English number plates and Doug gave a cheery "Good afternoon," as he walked by. The gentleman asked where he was going and Doug answered Spain. The man laughed and said that it was a long walk and would he like a drink of tea. Half and hour later the car set off with Doug in the backseat having accepted a lift to the South of France where the couple were heading. After a long drive they arrived at a villa still well short of the coast but the man who was called Mark said that he could stay the night with them and set off again in the morning. His wife Ellen gave him a meal and set up a little camp bed and Doug fell asleep thinking that his adventure had begun.

After breakfast the next day Doug started out again and managed to get another lift. Arriving at the coast he followed the shoreline seeing all the sights until he grew tired and sat down to eat a sandwich given by Ellen. As he studied the yachts in the harbour one stood out. From all the posters in his room he recognised the Spanish flag on one of the boats. He also knew that Spain was to the south and that was the way that he wanted to go. A young man was mopping the deck of the yacht. The man looked up and saw Doug watching him. "Are you lost," the man asked. Doug replied, "No, I was wondering whether that is a Spanish boat or not. You see I'm heading that way myself." The man stopped mopping and looked up. "Yes are you wanting a lift, you'll have to ask the captain," he said and nodded in the direction of the stern. "I'm just a hand and that is just the labourer aboard a vessel."

Moments later a man emerged from the stern and the hand talked to him in Spanish. The man smiled and to Doug in English, "So you are after a lift, can you wait table?" I don't know," replied Doug. "But I can try." "Better get your things and hop aboard then. He had a word with the hand and went back to the stern. Doug said that hadn't any things having lost them on the way down. The deck hand said to come aboard anyway. Doug had got his third free ride.

The yacht was around fifty feet in length and with a crew of three and a captain to look after just the two passengers the work was easy. Doug was given a pair of white shorts just like the crew but as the size was meant for a man they reached down to his ankles. With a length of white cord he hitched them up and started work. His first task was to learn how to lay the table in the correct manner and how to serve any guests and owner their food and drinks and afterwards to clear all the dishes without breaking anything. After eating in the crew quarters he had time off to watch the passing coast and as it became dark all the twinkling lights until he was given a bunk to sleep in. In the morning he found that the boat had docked during the night at the owner's home port of Cadiz in Southern Spain. After breakfast he thanked them for the trip and changed back into his shorts and left the yacht. Will thought about where to head for next. If he went north he was heading back from where he'd come from, and to the east was only Gibraltar which was British and they would send him back home so he didn't want to go there. That left the south but to do that he'd have to cross the sea to Morocco. Having decided he set off along the coast road hoping for a lift. For two day's he haunted the fishing docks looking for anything that showed signs of going further than the local area but found nothing. His food that he'd been given had run out and he was tired. On the third day a man spoke to him and asked if he had nothing to do as he'd seen Doug hanging around. Doug saw his chance and told him that he wanted a lift to Morocco but hadn't any money. The man asked if his parents couldn't provide the fare on the ferry and seemed interested when Doug said that he was on his own. He was told to wait as the fisherman talked with his fellow crew members, and finally invited Doug aboard. The fishing boat was old and not in good condition with a lot of rust and decay and some water sloshing about at the bottom of the boat, still it wasn't far and it was free.

The boat was slow and the engine sounded rough as though it needed a good service but they arrived in the early evening at a port called Tetuan in Morocco. The man told Doug to come with him and he would find him a bed for the night. An unmade track led to a mud brick built building on the outskirts of the port. Doug was told to wait outside as the man entered. After twenty minutes he came out with another man who took a look at Doug and nodded his head. The men went back inside and then the fisherman left saying to Doug to wait as the other man would look after him. A door opened and a woman beckoned to him and took him inside where he was fed and then led to a bed for the night. In the morning the woman took him to the yard and gave him some soap and a towel and showed him where a tap was. He'd nearly finished washing when the man appeared with another man who took a look at Doug and after a discussion between them motioned Doug to come with them. He wrapped the towel around his waist to follow them when the woman snatched it away and pushed him out. A wagon was outside and the other man picked up Doug and threw him onto the back. He climbed on board and the wagon set off leaving Doug's clothing behind. After an hour they pulled up in a yard surrounded by buildings in the port of Casablanca. There Doug was told to get out and shown into a room containing eight beds. Four of the beds were occupied by woman wearing a one piece garment of muslin that was so thin it could be described as see through. The door slammed shut and a key turned in a lock, he was a prisoner.

For two day's they waited until on the third day they were joined by four more woman and two men. Doug had an uncomfortable night wrapped in a blanket as his bed had been taken over by the men. Some food was handed to the woman that was to be shared out but it was almost uneatable. In the morning the same food was given to them until they were suddenly ordered out and onto the wagon. The sides were covered to block any view and two men climbed aboard both carrying rifles. The drove for ten minutes to a large building full of people and there took to a room to wait.

Doug was taken out and led by the arm around twenty tables while the people prodded and poked him while he was still naked and then taken back into the room. The woman was taken out one by one but wearing a number. Afterwards Doug was pushed out again and bidding began. He finally realised that the place was an auction house and they were selling slaves, and he was one.

The wagon bumped and bounced over a sandy stone strewed track without any signs or dwellings. It was hours since the auction and Doug along with four women and four black men had been taken from the building and ordered into the wagon. The wagon had left the town and soon the road ended and the track had begun. Doug was thirsty and hungry but no food was given and it didn't look as if the wagon was going to stop any time soon. The group were seated upon some crates that looked as though they could be food supplies and then were some jerry cans that had a petrol smell. They were obviously heading to a base somewhere but not in a particularly hurry. The guards were relaxed but he dismissed any chance of rushing them and escaping as being impractical.

Doug woke up with a start. The wagon had stopped and someone was shouting at him in a foreign language but as the others were leaving he followed. He was besides a long low building in a large compound made from mud brick walls and having an iron gate at one end. Three boys were watching the wagon, two were of Africa appearance and one was an Arab. All three of the boys were naked. The two guards ushered them into what appeared to be a nightclub having tables and chairs and equipped with a plush carpet. Overhead hung expensive lighting in the form of chandeliers

At one of tables a large burly man stood and came over to the group and after lining them up and inspecting them dismissed them with a wave of his hand. The group were taken around to the rear of the building and housed in a large room. Doug was led off to a room as big as a large cupboard that held a mattress and a small table. On the table was a pot of cream and an artist brush. He was pushed into the room and the door locked. It stayed lock until evening when he was taken out to be given some food and then into the nightclub where he and the other boys were put to work. They helped with restocking the bar with mostly soft drinks and putting the chairs around the tables from where they had been stacked, and stetting up pipes for the clients to smoke. Afterwards he got the chance to have a wash and to talk to the other boys but only one could speak a little English. They told him to stay clear of Abdul the owner as he was a nasty man. Doug was going to ask what they did when they were called back into the club and the talking had to stop.

Every thing was ready for the clients but they wouldn't come until late in the evening. The group were all locked in the large rear room where one of the girls approached Doug. "Are you English," she asked. "We don't see many around here." She told of owing money that she borrowed for her fathers funeral and being sold to the slave dealer and then to Abdul to work here in the brothel. Doug had heard of brothels but wasn't quiet sure what went on in them. The woman who said that her name was Maria gave him a sad look. "You'll find out tonight, that's why you've been brought here."

The full implications of the brothel sank in to Doug. "You mean that I will have to…" He didn't say the last words but Maria just nodded her head.

It was the evening when they were let out of the room. The women had changed into their colourful but nearly transparent gowns but the boy's were still naked. He was told that he'd to collect tokens each time that he took a client and he'd to collect thirty a month or get a beating from Abdul and that's why the other boys were interested in who was being brought in to work because the prettier the boy meant that they would get fewer tokens, and with Doug having a light skin they thought that he'd be the first choice. There wasn't anything that Doug could do about his skin and he didn't want to be here.

The first guests started to arrive just after eight. By ten the compound was full of cars but no English. Doug wanted to let someone know of his plight but was out of luck. Around eleven Doug was serving bottles of cola or orange juice to anyone who called. As he walked around the nightclub he would be grabbed and fondled by anyone who wanted to give him a quick grope and he just had to stand there and take it. Suddenly Abdul grabbed his arm and led him away to his little room. He was force to his knees on the mattress but resisted and tried to get up. Abdul swung his fist and knocked Doug so hard that landed on to his back with his head spinning. Abdul pulled him back onto his knees then pushed his head down. He dipped the artist brush into the cream and rammed it up Doug's bum so hard that he shrieked out in pain. Abdul carried on with the brush and then came a knock at the door. One of the men that had been fondling Doug stood there and Abdul left the room. The man pulled Doug up and sat him onto his knee and then started to kiss and caress him. His mouth tasted of Garlic and Doug wanted to pull away but was fearful of Abdul returning and really giving him a beating and so had to put up with the man. When he'd had his fill Doug was pushed back onto his knees and waited for the inevitable thing that he knew would happen. Sure enough moments later came that pain again as the man entered him. Doug was almost crying when the man had finished.

He stood and dressed and then gave Doug a token, smiled and left the room. Doug's first ordeal was over but he had to return into the nightclub to try and get more clients or else.

About two in the morning the club began to quieten down as the clients started to leave. The eldest of the two African boys began to sob as he'd only taken three tokens for his nights work and he knew that Abdul would expect double or would think that the boy wasn't trying and that would lead to a beating. Doug handed his tokens in to be counted, he had six which for the first time was considered good as he had yet to learn the knack of enticing men. He was taken to the large room to sleep.

Maria came to see him as she thought that he may like some company after his first ordeal. They discussed ways to get away from the compound and Abdul and the life they have been forced into, but it was going to be difficult. The only way from the compound was by means of the gate which had an armed guard at all times. They could tunnel but as they were locked in during the daytime any tunnel had to start from this one room and travel for fifty feet or more and when they got out what then? They were in the middle of the desert a hundred miles from any town without transport. The supply wagon left once every week but not until late afternoon after the midday heat and all the slaves were locked away. The only other car belonged to Abdul and only he had the keys and the guard knew that nobody else drove it and he wouldn't open the gate. Doug did some quick reckoning and counted the number of men working for Abdul. "He has six in the building and one on the gate with only two men going with the wagon, plus three cooks and a maintenance man who we don't know if they're just workmen or would they fight for Abdul. That could leave six armed counting Abdul and three or four who we don't know if they will take sides and that's what we will face from any uprising. We need the four Black slaves that came with me. What are they doing?"

"They're building a second wall just outside of the first. If they get it finished then this place will be like a fortress and we'll never get out, but they too are locked in just as we are. When they work they are under an armed guard." Maria replied. They both fell quiet and Doug lay down to get some sleep.

The scrapping noise told Doug that the door bolt was being withdrawn. The door opened and a guard entered followed by the maintenance man. The man pointed to Doug and the guard beckoned to him to come out. He was taken by the maintenance man up to the workshop at the end of the long block. The workshop had a square metal table, a drilling machine, a lathe and a grinding machine next to a saw. At the very end was the man's bed. Doug gathered that he must live in the workshop. The man put a leather apron on Doug and showed him how to load the saw with sections of angle iron to be cut into lengths. These must be for a new gate to go into the new wall that was being built. After cutting, the lengths had to have all the sharp edges taken off with the grinding machine. Doug worked for an hour when a sudden bang from the saw told him that the saw blade had broken and needed to be replaced. The man took out a new blade and started to fit it to the saw throwing the old pieces into a bin holding some scrap metal. After he tried the new blade Doug had to restart the saw watched by the man who was sitting on the table just behind Doug. The saw finished the cut and Doug was going to release the clamp when he was grabbed from behind and pulled onto the man's knees. Doug didn't know what to do as he'd no idea whether he was dealing with a guard or just a workman. A hand caressed his leg moving up under the apron and Doug moved to resist it but his hand was knocked away. The apron strings were loosened and the hand moved higher to stroke his genitals when Abdul suddenly entered having arrived back early. The maintenance man sprang to his feet dropping Doug to the sandy floor but as he did Doug felt something sharp beneath his feet. He grasped it and realised that it was part of a broken saw blade. The guard took him out from the workshop and back to the large sleeping hut. When the door closed he crossed over to where Maria slept and dropped the blade on her blanket. "Do you think that this might help?" He asked.

Two day's later Doug was called by the guard supervising the four African men building the wall. The guard told him to collect the water bucket and fill it with water for the builders. Doug did so and took the water outside the compound and around to where the men were working. The guard was lolling some distance away and shouted that he wanted a drink before the men. This suited Doug because he could have longer to tell of the blade. He return and as the first man was taking a drink quickly told of having the means of escape and be ready as soon as Abdul and the wagon left the compound. Doug picked up the empty water bucket and politely asked if they had enough and the guard said that they had and to return to the compound.

The wagon left for supplies and more fuel for the generator. Abdul drove out shortly afterward. All the slaves were locked away to rest after their nights work, and everything was quiet. Maria took the blade and began to saw through the bolt. No guards would be stationed at this side of the compound and soon they were free. Maria asked the others to remain here and she and Doug went to the room of the African men. After a small knock they answered. Maria began to saw the bolt and that too offered little in the way of resistance. Maria began to outline her plan to escape. First of all we need weapons and a good place to start was the cookhouse where the cooks would have plenty of sharp knifes. This early in the afternoon the cooks would be resting as it was too early to start the evening meal. The men simply walked in and picked up the best weapons that they could find. A length of cord on a reel was just what they needed to tie the hands and feet of the three men and warn them that any noise from them and they would get a knife in the ribs. They needed a gun and thought that the man on the gate should be their target. If they captured him then that would leave only four to deal with before the return of the Abdul and the wagon. The plan was to use Doug as a decoy with the water bucket again. He would take the bucket of water and make as though he was again going outside to take the bucket to the workers. One of the men would then sneak up on him as Doug distracted him. Doug filled the bucket and also placed a small knife in the bottom. When he was ready he set off and one of the men also moved going around the rear of the generator. Doug neared the guard who stopped listening to his radio and regarded Doug as he approached. "Taking water out?" he questioned speaking in good English. "I didn't know they were working. Just a minute they aren't outside, what's going on?" Doug hesitated for a moment as he realised the man had addressed him in English. Just then the guard spotted the black slave coming at him carrying a knife. He turned and raised his rifle as Doug, having picked up the small knife stabbed him in the arm causing him to drop his weapon. The guard snarled at Doug and stooped to retrieve his gun but the slave was on him and the knife sliced into his ribs. They dragged him out of sight and retreated back to the buildings now armed with the man's rifle.

"I think the easiest way of getting the other men out is to turn off the generator. The building will get as hot as hell without the air conditioning and they will have to come out and investigate." Doug said. They agreed that they had to get them out before Abdul returned and if they were looking at the generator they'd be unprepared and vulnerable for an attack. The generator was at the top of the site in a shed without a door to let out any heat build up but the shed next to it housed all the fuel and that did have a door. If it was left ajar anyone inside could see all the compound and ambush anybody coming near.

The switch was thrown and all the lights turn off. It wasn't very long before the guard emerged trying to find the fault with the lights or the light switches. He finally left the nightclub and walked up to the generator shed and entered not noticing the door to the fuel depot slowly open, it was his last mistake.

The group met at the fuel shed to discuss their next move. The black men were former soldiers and felt that they now had the upper hand with two rifles and the element of surprise and they wanted to go on the attack. The guard's rooms were at the rear of the nightclub and the only way in was to go through the club as there wasn't a door to the rear meaning if the guard was in his room he was trapped. They decided to get down there as quickly as possible. The two men with the rifles separated with one going through the club and the other going to the rear passing the slave room and in through the bottom door. When they were ready the first men knocked on the guard's door and after the guard replied said that he was wanted at the generator. The door opened but the guard had his rifle at the ready and fired as the soldier sprung back. The bullet just missed but the second soldier fired through the door hitting the guard who dropped his weapon and then the first soldier opened fired and the guard was fatally wounded. That just left one who heard the firing and came out ready to fire. They began a fire fight between them until the third soldier picked up the just killed man's rifle and raced around the building to come into the rear of the nightclub trapping the guard in a cross fire. He retreated to his room and closed the door as the soldiers advanced. They called on him to give up but got a shot through the door as a reply. Both men opened fire in return and then all was quiet until they kicked the door down and found the man dead. With all the guards dead the slaves were freed but not the workmen. A fierce debate started between the soldiers and the slaves as to what to do with the prisoners. They must have known about the slaves and didn't inform the authorities and it could be said that they co-operated with Abdul because without their help he couldn't have run the place.

"This is getting us nowhere, let's decide later meanwhile there's still Abdul and two of the guards with the truck to deal with," she said using a mixture of French and English. "All slaves leave the compound, there's going to be bullets flying about." The women and the boys went outside to keep the wall between them and of the fighting. All they had to do was to wait. An hour later a cloud of dust was seen in the distance, Abdul was coming.

The gate was closed as it would be with the guard on duty. He would open it as he saw Abdul's car and close it when it had entered the compound unless the wagon was following and then he would wait. Today they had to let both through and get the gate closed before they could leave. The dust got neared and the watcher suddenly shouted that there were two cars coming with the wagon behind. Maria shouted to let them through and open fire on the wagon with the two guards.

Abdul led the way through the gate followed by the man who owned the slave house that sold Doug. Abdul must have known that something wasn't right as he skidded to a halt and half got out of his car with the slave trader pulling alongside. The wagon entered and came to a stop by the cookhouse to unload the new supplies. Immediately the two guards came under fire from the generator shed. The first volley from such a close range was fatal and the guards fell dead. The driver put up his hands as a sign of surrender but Abdul fired his revolver and jumped back into his car to escape but the gate had been closed. He reversed down to the night-club and abandoned his car running into the club. Moments later he emerged with a machine gun and sprayed the compound forcing everyone to take cover. Maria shouted at the men at the generator shed to encircle the nightclub and create crossfire between the two parties. The Slave trader tried to join Abdul but was too slow. He drew a pistol from his car but as soon as he left he was caught by a bullet and fell to the ground. Abdul tried to build a barricade but was being attacked on three sides as one of the men had come through the rear door and opened fire. Another man ran around to the rear and two men were at the front. Soon the firing stopped and Abdul was no more.

Everyone was rejoicing as they were now free. Maria was more practical and ran over to where Abdul lay. After making sure that he was dead she took his keys and went over to the Slave Trade and picked up his pistol. While searching to see if he'd any more ammunition with him she found a bulge in his robe. She investigated and discovered that he was wearing a body belt. After taking it off it produced a large amount of cash which she kept for later to share out between all the slaves. With the key's from Abdul she searched the office safe and found more cash and a lot of documents that the police would be interested in. The next thing to do would be to decide what to do with the other people in the compound, the cooks and the wagon driver and the maintenance man. Some wanted to kill them and others wanted to hand them to the police as they were part of what was going on and it was only with their help that it could have taken place. In the end it was decided to take them out into the desert and leave them to walk back. They were loaded into the truck and told to strip as their clothing was needed for the slaves. The truck drove for thirty miles and then the men were ordered out to walk back. With no clothing and nothing on their feet and no water it would be an even chance if they got back.

The soldiers decided to head south hoping to get to South Africa so they took the Slave Traders car and the boys along with a share of the food and some extra fuel. Maria gave them their share of the cash and they set off. The wagon returned and the woman wanted to go to Libya. They shared what clothing they could find and with extra fuel, food and cash they too set off. After searching through the available clothing that was left Doug found a small tunic that had been discarded by the women as being too small but it just fitted Doug. Maria said that the place should be destroyed to prevent it being used again. The fuel store held lots of jerry cans full of fuel and Doug started to douse everything in petrol. He did the fuel store after filling the car and putting two extra cans in the boot, and then did the generator and the kitchen while Maria did the nightclub. They packed the food and their cash in the car and drove a safe distance and then returned on foot to set fire to the place. Soon everything was ablaze as they drove north and away from the inferno.

Maria had somewhere to go as she drove north but Doug wasn't sure of his destination. He always had it mind to see New York and the Empire State building but that was as far as it got. Now he was on the road to Casablanca and not knowing what to do next. After two hours driving they caught up with the wagon. It was stopped outside a little market on the road and all of the women had gone to buy suitable clothing. Maria and Doug joined them and Doug managed to buy a pair of shorts and a t-shirt.

Maria pulled up at the police station in Casablanca to tell of the Slave Dealer and Abdul's brothel and their fate. She left the documents that were in the safe but didn't mention the cash because she had a feeling that any money that she handed over would somehow disappear. Doug waited outside in the car as he had decided to travel on with Maria. Setting off again they took the road to Algeria but cut inland to avoid the frontier post as neither Maria nor Doug had a passport. The next day Maria reached her home town of Algiers but Doug decided to carry on through Libya and on to see the pyramids in Egypt. Maria took him to a place where a lot of the wagon's stopped overnight before carrying on to further destinations. Through casual enquiries she managed to isolate a place where a small group of wagons were heading to Tunisia which was on the way. Maria told Doug to ask the drivers for a lift in the morning and then climbed into the car and said goodbye and drove away. When the drivers returned Doug used sign language to ask for a lift but was refused. The first three wagons pulled out and as the fourth and last one started someone walked in front of the wagon and the drive had to slam on his brakes and started to shout at the pedestrian. Doug saw a chance and climbed aboard and hid in a pile of sacks. After about four hours of travel they came to the border but after a brief inspection passed through and continued their journey. Another six hours brought them to a little town called Medenine and this was their destination for the trucks pulled in to a large depot and a group of men started unloading. Doug had by this time fallen asleep in the bottom of the wagon. A cry went out as they found him still sleeping and he was dragged to his feet and dropped over the side of the wagon into the arms of a big burly man who seemed to be the foreman. He was taken to an office and questioned but didn't understand the language and so couldn't answer. A van drew up and he was pushed inside and taken to a row of dwellings in a back street. As they drew up a woman came out of the dwelling and an argument started about Doug but what was said he didn't know but could tell that the woman was unhappy about him being there. Finally she took him into the house where there was six other children playing and making noise. Doug thought these must be her children and that she had enough to do without looking after a stowaway.

She gave him some type of gruel and a spoon and left him to eat but he was too tired and after a few spoonfuls he was nearly asleep. The woman came and saw that he hadn't eaten the gruel and became very angry. She took hold of Doug and started to lash out and slap him while shouting at him but he couldn't understand her. She took hold of his shirt and pulled it over his head, next his new pants were stripped of along with his new sandals and his underwear. He was dragged outside where a dog sat in a large wire cage. The door was opened and he was pushed in with the dog and the catch was fastened.

The cage sat in a small backyard and the walls radiated all the heat of the day. The temperature must have been over eighty and there wasn't any water to drink. The dog was an old mongrel and covered in fleas. It was sitting on a little bit of old carpet covering the floor and appeared to be regarding Doug with wonder. As long as it didn't bite him or attack him for invading its territory Doug didn't mind. He was stuck until they came and took him out from the cage and so he may as well finish his sleep. He curled up and closed his eyes.

Doug awoke from his sleep to find that it was morning but at least it had cooled down a little. The door to his cage opened and a dish of something brown was pushed towards him and another dish of water was placed alongside. He wasn't given a spoon or anything to eat with and so dipped his finger in and tasted it. The food had a peculiar taste and as the dog had been given the same looking food in a similar dish he wondered whether he was given a dish of dog food. The door clanged shut and he heard the catch drop and once again he was shut in for who knew how long. He tried some more of the food but even the dog had ignored it and had gone back to sleep. Doug curled up and he too fell asleep again. He awoke as the fleas started to bite as the heat built in the yard. Doug was slapping at his legs and the dog started to growl as it thought that it was going to be slapped but stopped as a flea was dispatched and the dog appeared to realise that he had a friend. The mongrel gave a small wag of its tail and edge towards Doug who gave it a pat on its head and from then on they were friends.

The day dragged on and heat started to build up and one of the children came and took the dog out from the cage and tied a length of rope to its collar. Another of the children beckoned to Doug to come from the cage and as he did a piece of rope was tied around his neck and he was led to an outhouse that contained a hole in the ground. He gathered that this must be their toilet facility and they wanted him to use it. As he needed the toilet he obliged and then he was taken to a water tap and given a tin mug to douse himself with water and it was back to the cage and locked up again.

The other children went back into the house and an older boy came out and looked at him. Doug saw that the boy had on some new clothes, his clothes, his t-shirt and new shorts that he'd just bought three days ago and it didn't look as though he was going to be given them back. At mid morning the mother came and took out the dog and led it into the room of the house and that was the last he saw of the dog.

A week passed and Doug was still in the cage and one morning as the door closed the catch didn't engage as it usually did. As the door to the house was usually open to let the air circulate he made a dash for freedom and ran from the house and onto the road. He then discovered that the house was only one of half a dozen and beyond was only the desert waste; there wasn't anywhere to run to. The only thing to do was to put some distance between the house and him and then hope that some kind of transport would come along and pick him up. He set off at a run keeping up a steady pace but not having any footwear was hard on his feet and he had to slow down. The sound of an engine gave him a little hope of a wagon coming along but instead of a wagon it was the van in which he'd been brought. Doug made for the desert away from the road and hoped that the driver hadn't seen him but the van turned of the road and towards him Doug turned once more as another car was following and that too turned to cut him off. He could now see that it was hopeless and that he couldn't keep outrunning them. He sat down and waited for them to catch up. The man got out of the van and grabbed him by the arm and in one movement pulled him over his knees and gave Doug a good spanking. With Doug now in tears he was taken away from the house to a local smithy. After a few words with the blacksmith the smithy took a rod heating it up and bending it into a circle. He measured Doug's neck and cut the rod to length. Doug was made to bend over the anvil and a length of chain was threaded onto the bent rod and the two ends were hammered together and for good measure where the ends met he put on a spot weld. Doug was back in the van and soon back in his cage but this time wearing a collar and chain. The last link of the chain was then padlocked onto the cage so even if the door was left open then Doug was still chained up and couldn't escape even if there was any place to run to.

Two week passed and nobody had come to see him. The children in the house ignored him except for his twice daily visit to the lavatory and even that was getting shorter with a savage pull on the chain if he didn't hurry. The food was mainly the grey gruel with a dish of water. Doug was sure that this was dog food that they were using up as there was no sign of the mongrel dog coming back. Then one day two men came to the door and one man pointed at him and said something to the other and then both left. Two day's more passed and then the van was back. Doug was taken from his cage and put into the rear of the van still naked and with the collar and chain. Nothing was said about his clothing or the money that he had brought and he thought that he wouldn't see either again. They set off going down the coast road but turned off towards a little fishing port consisting of a beach and two boats. The boats looked like Dhows the Arab sailing craft. Doug was ordered out and taken on board one of the vessels and once more his chain was padlock in the bow out of the way from the crew. It was late in the afternoon and the sun was going down. When he was in the cage the walls radiated heat and kept him warm at night but now chained in the bow of a boat with a wind coming from the sea he felt cold but there wasn't any cover and he wasn't given any thing to wear or eat. He just had to suffer and shiver throughout the night. In the morning he was given a bowl of rice and a hot mug of tea and then the boat set off heading out to sea. Around two miles out the crew started fishing and ignored Doug. Around three in the afternoon the nets were hauled in and the boat headed to port but not their own port but one a little way further down the coast. As they neared Doug could see a car that appeared to be waiting and wondered if it was waiting for him. A crunch from the keel told him they were on the beach and he looked to see if anyone came from the car. The crew unlocked the padlock and took Doug to a house where it appeared that he was expected. He was handed over to another man and the crewman left. Inside the house four men were waiting and he was grabbed and lifted onto one of the men's knees where he was fondled. By this time Doug knew better than try to resist because that would only mean getting a slap or a punch for his trouble and so he just let the man get on with it. Sure enough the man picked him up and took him into the next room where he proceeded to rape Doug and he was followed in turn by the other men. When they had finished with him he was taken outside to another cage and locked in.

The next morning he was transferred to another little port further down the coast and put into a warehouse containing sacks of herbs and spices. His chain was wrapped around a post, locked and after being given a vegetable stew he was left alone. He spent the rest of the day watching the workmen loading the various kinds of spices and fulfilling orders. Some wagons came with goods others took goods away. At night he was fed and given a blanket and left alone again until the morning when he was taken out to a wagon and left the warehouse. The wagon went to the little port and a relay of men loaded a Dhow. When they had finish he was handed to the captain of the Dhow and the boat put to sea. The boat sailed west along the coast and the next day put into Tripoli and unloaded some sacks and took some onboard. At the next port of Misurata they did the same and although Doug was in open view being naked and chained to the deck nobody took the slightest notice. A week later one of the crew pointed to shore and said that was the port of Alexandria and Doug knew from his maps that he'd reached Egypt. The put in to the port and unloaded the rest of the cargo. A crew man went ashore and returned with a man. Doug was handed over and led to a house where yet another cage was waiting. As the door opened Doug obliged by entering the cage without being told and sat down thinking that if he cooperated with his captors then he may get better treatment. His plan seemed to work as he was given food and two blankets and once fed he settled down to sleep.

Mr R Jones was a self made man and had come through the war as a Major in the US Army Air Force. But while he served his country his company was doing very well serving the armaments needs of the troops and as a result had finish more wealthy than at the start of the war. He was now in semi retirement and had decided to see something of the world in his luxury yacht a vessel of sixty feet in length and having both sails and an engine, equipped with a crew of eight and a captain. Mr Jones' wife loved travel and her passion had been somewhat curtailed during the hostilities and now they had decided to have a world cruise. Having just finished cruising in the Mediterranean they intended to go through the Suez canal but the captain had informed Mr Jones that they needed to put into port for some supplies and so they had put into Alexandria and although they were in part of the port where tourist don't usually go they decided to have a look around while the vessel was restocked. Mr Jones had taken the precaution of arming himself in case of any trouble but every-thing was very normal.

It was getting near the time to return to the ship when two men approach and one man asked in English if they would like to buy a slave. Mr Jones was just brushing them aside when the other man mentioned that the slave in ques-tion was an American boy. Mr Jones stopped in his tracks. The mention of an American boy caught his attention and he asked if they were sure the boy was American. He said that he would see the boy but not here on the dockside but on his yacht. The men said that they would bring the boy out to the boat but not let him board until they had receive the money, Mr Jones agreed.

Doug was woken roughly from his sleep as he was pulled out of the cage. A car drew up and a voice told him in English to get in and as soon as he did so it set off weaving through the backstreets of the port and ending at the dock side where a small skiff waited. He seated in the bow of the boat and the end of his chain was padlocked around the seat. Two men climbed in and the boat was pushed off heading towards the big yacht that was anchored in the harbour. They reached the yacht and a crew man informed the captain who in turn informed Mr Jones. The skiff kept just clear of the yacht but close enough so that a conversation could be carried on between them. Mr Jones asked Doug who he was and where he'd come from. Doug was told to stand up so that they could see that he wasn't an Arab boy and they could also see the chain that he wore. Doug told them he thought that his father was American and his mother English and their boat had sunk after a collision in the Mediterranean he had been taken to England because that's where the rescue boat was heading and put into an orphanage. He wanted to go to America but got kidnapped and had been used in a brothel. Mr Jones discussed the situation with the captain and Mrs Jones and they decided that the boy's story sounded true and they should try and buy his freedom. After asking what price they wanted for the boy and being given a ridicules figure negotiations began. A price was finally agreed and Doug was exchanged for a sum of money. He was free once more.

Doug was taken below to have the collar removed and to find some clothing to fit him. He was fed and allowed to rest as the yacht headed towards the canal and join the queue of waiting boats for their turn to enter the canal at Port Said. After leaving the port the canal stretched out before them but at each side it was mostly just a sandy waste land and with not may landmark Doug went below and was given the job of mopping the floor until the Captain and Mr Jones sent for him to be questioned about his background and how he had become a slave. He told them as much as he knew which wasn't a lot. Just after the war a British destroyer came across a fishing boat that was slowly sinking. Upon investigating they found a box containing the ships papers which turned out to be false. Along with the papers were some passports of a man and women and these passports were also false. The passport photographs were of two white people but they had not been traced and their names were unknown. There were bullet holes in the boat and it looked as though an attack had taken place. As they were about to leave a noise was made by a baby and that was me. The man who found me was named Douglas and I was called Douglas's baby and then just

Douglas. My surname is the name of the orphanage where I was placed. Doug then told of boarding the wrong boat and his adventures since then. They did add that it's possible that his father was American because the false papers were written using American English and as they found some papers written in a women's handwriting and in both English and French the mother could either one. Doug added that he didn't want to go back to the orphanage but wanted to see something of the world.

The yacht passed through the port of Suez and out into the Red Sea and on to India and the City of Bombay. The travelled to Ceylon and then up to Hong Kong in China and then back down to Australia and New Zealand and finally across the Pacific Ocean to Panama and through the canal to the Caribbean and then up to the United States. Doug had wanted to see the world and had seen a great more than he expected when he'd taken the boat to France. The docked in New York very close to the sky scrapers. The authorities had to be informed about Doug but he was granted temporary status as crew. Mr Jones took him to the Empire State Building and then bought him a ticket to ride the elevator to the top where some photographs were taken. The British Authorities were informed and said that he would be given a passport to enable him to fly home. Two weeks later he back in the home recounting all his adventures to the other boys and girls and showing him at the top of the sky scraper. Those in charge at the home gave him a good talking to but knew that it was falling on deaf ears. They were telling him of all the dangers when he'd already been through those dangers, and had the experiences of a life time because of them.

A letter arrived from Mr Jones addressed to him at the home. It told of how much they missed him and would he consent to being adopted by him and Mrs Jones? Doug now Douglas Jones was last heard of living in America.

CHAPTER 5

JACK

Jack was in the hotel having his breakfast and savouring his first day of freedom. He had arrived just two days earlier with his parents and had been doing the tourist thing with his mother and farther while they waited for the yacht to finish loading. His father's friend and business colleague was taking them cruising on a long trip down to Brazil and maybe Argentina and then back up to the Panama Canal and through to the Pacific Ocean and up the coast to San Francisco, but Jack wasn't going with them as he suffered from sea sickness. Jack, instead of cruising was going to tour the states and do all the sights and after crossing the country meet up with his parents at his grandmother's home in San Francisco and today was the day, the first day of freedom.

Jack finished his breakfast wandered back to his room to shower and finish packing his backpack. He left out some new Versace underwear his mother had insisted that he took, and his passport and money and a train ticket to Buffalo the nearest stop to the falls but his parents would leave at Baltimore where the boat was based.

After his shower he changed into the underwear and with new socks and trainers along with a new sports shirt he was ready to begin his adventure. The passport was safely stowed along with his grandmother's address and spare cash and traveller's cheques and a complete change of clothes. In the lobby his parents were also waiting for a taxi and then they all climbed in and set off to the station. The train followed the Hudson River down which the yacht would soon sail. At Baltimore Jack said his goodbyes and he was free.

Buffalo was an industrial town and apart from all the grain silo's there wasn't a lot that interested him. A small park afforded him a place to rest and then to find a hotel for the night. He slipped off the pack and closed his eyes for a moment and opened them to find two very pretty girls sat on the seat besides him. He soon got chatting and he was asked if he would like to go with them to a party. Jack was fifteen and looked young so he was a bit flatted to have picked up two pretty girls. The told him they would take him to a youth hostel where he could leave his pack and then he could enjoy himself. Jack agreed but then a peel of thunder sounded and the rain poured down drenching them before they could reach shelter.

The three booked in to the hostel and he was told that a drying room was available in the basement but that the hostel wasn't responsible for any losses of clothing. The girls had an idea that if he bought a small lock and chain they thread the chain through the clothing and it would be safe, and Jack agreed. A small shop sold him a small lock and some strong but thin chain which was used to secure his clothes. That night he had a great time and drunk a little more than he ought but he was thinking what the night may bring.

At eight in the morning he awoke with a headache to find he was lying across the bed in the hostel. His clothing along with his passport and money and the cheques were missing and also the girls. It was now obvious that he had been set up and robbed. The little keys to the lock in the basement were still in the bathroom where he had emptied the pockets of his jeans. With a towel wrapped around his waist he made his way down and much to his relief they were all still there being much too wet to steal or the girls didn't find the keys. He dressed and set out to see if he could find out where he girls had gone. They had talked about going together to see the falls and so he headed for Niagara Falls. With no money for a train ticket he managed to hitch a ride to the falls and started to look around but didn't see the girls. After two hours he gave up and sat down what to do next. He didn't want to go to the police and admit two little girls had duped him and stolen his cash and all he had was a pack with a lock and chain and that was only because the pack had an English flag painted on the back. It was then that he remembered that the address of his grandmother was in his wallet and he didn't know it as he'd only been there once when he was very small. He decided that he might as well carry on with his holiday the best he could and so headed towards where route 66 started and that meant getting a lift to Chicago.

It was long way and the lifts were thin on the ground. He managed one short lift and then got lucky and got a long one all the way to Cleveland where he sheltered in a barn. The next morning he rested along his way on a park bench and a man asked him what the flag on his backpack was. Jack told him in was an English flag also told him of starting his holiday and being robbed and of making his way to California and trying to see some sights along the route. The man said that he was waiting for his wife and if he liked he would give him a lift to the other side of town. Jack was grateful especially when he bought Jack a meal to help him along. One hour later he was walking along the highway with a full belly and a $20 note in his pocket courtesy of the man's wife who donated it to help him along his way. Jack decided to hide the note and save it for any emergency that might arise. He lifted the bottom cover in his backpack and slid the note beneath it. He walked through the afternoon and didn't get any lifts. By late evening it started to grow dark and rain clouds were gathering and still he couldn't get a ride. He was standing besides the road when a silver coloured van pulled in and a black man leaned from the window and asked if he wanted a ride. Just then a first rain drop splashed onto his face and that helped to him to make up his mind and so he accepted. The man told him to get in and Jack opened the sliding door noticing some faded lettering on the vans side. It had probably been a workman's at some stage of its life. Inside were two black youths. One was sitting on a large tool chest and the other a boy, was sitting on the floor and Jack joined him on the floor as the set off. The boy asked Jack where he was going to and Jack replied Chicago. The youth then asked what was in the backpack and was told nothing. The boy must have taken Jack's answer to be a kind of insult for he made a grab for the pack but Jack pulled it back. Suddenly the other youth sprang onto Jack and pushed a large knife against his throat. Jack thought for a moment that he was going to cut his throat but the youth just said that the boy wanted to see his pack. Jack let loose his grip on the pack and the boy opened it and tipped out the only thing that it contained which were the thin chain and the little brass lock. The boy seemed disappointed that there weren't any valuables in the pack and asked what the chain was for. Jack told him it was to protect his clothing to stop them from being stolen in the hostel. The boy could see that jack was wearing good quality clothes and that he had a vest that was full of holes and a pair or old shorts that had a tear and were dirty and stained.

"I bet that you'd like to give me that shirt cos I aint got one." The boy pointed to Jack's shirt. The youth pressed the blade of the knife harder against Jacks throat and snarled "Tek it off." Reluctantly Jack pulled up the bottom of the shirt realising that he was being robbed and that is why the van had stopped in the first place. For brief moment Jack thought about grabbing the knife when it was removed from his throat to allow his shirt to be pulled over his head but he was told to lie down and the youth then knelt upon him leaving no opportunity to grab the knife and the shirt was removed.

"Wow he got Versace underwear on." Jack felt his vest being pulled up and that too followed his shirt. Something dropped over his head, it was the chain from his pack that the boy had made a loop with and now his arms were being chained behind his back. The chain cut into his wrists and neck but the youth pushed them higher and then put on the little brass lock, Jack was helpless. He was rolled over onto his back as the boy sat on his legs and removed his trainer and sport socks. Now the youth reached for Jack's belt and then he felt the zip of his Jeans being lowered. He was being stripped naked and couldn't do anything about it. The youth opened the tool chest and brought out a length of rope and tied Jacks ankles and propped him against the side of the van. The boy removed his tattered vest and picked up Jacks vest. Soon the boy was fully dressed in Jacks clothes and trainers and had kicked his old clothes to the rear of the van. Jack wondered what he was going to be given to wear but that appeared to be nothing making him a little concerned about what would happen to him.

The van drove on for a while and then stopped as the youth and the boy joined those in the front. Shortly they set off again but going more slowly than before and occasionally pausing as though looking for something. They pulled off down a small road that was used to serve the few farms in the area and stopped besides a field where Jack had the rope take from his ankles and then frog marched into the field and up to a large advertisement standing on two large logs. He was told to lie down and then tied by his ankles once again to the logs where he was left. The van turned around and left leaving him in the dark. In the far distance he could see the flash of car headlights but when they had passed it was pitch black. The first thing he had to do was to the road as it was already becoming cold. Turning around he followed the rope to where it was tied and with his teeth began working on the knot. After what seemed an age it finally loosened and he was free of his tether. He reasoned that the bill board would face the road and headed directly away rolling to his left and then his right trying to keep more or less in a straight line. He was cold and muddy but daren't stop and had to make the road. A small dip in the field and suddenly he was falling. There was a drainage ditch between the road and the field and he had fallen into it. He went under the muddy bottom of the ditch and fought to regain his footing but it like a swamp and just didn't allow any solid place to put his feet. His head broke the surface and thankfully he paused while he got his breath back and then stood up like a big black slug rising from a swamp. A smell of rotting vegetation arose as tried to clear the black mud from his face by rubbing himself on the grass at the side of the ditch. He tried to move but with the ditch being so deep and him trailing a rope through the sticky mud it wasn't very easy as he could only move him feet two to three inches at any one time. A car passed and for a brief moment he could see along the bank and saw a place where the track crossed into the field. A large pipe had been laid along the ditch and the track had been built over the ditch to allow tractors a way in and possibly for him a way out. He started to edge towards the pipe but it over an hour to reach and then he had to brace his legs between the pipe and the bank to push up to the road level and then roll clear. He was sweating and breathing hard but knew that soon he would cool down and then feel the cold. Another car passed by before he could rise and show himself but he determined to let any more see him and rose into a kneeling position and waited. He saw the flash of head-lights coming along the road and saw a little truck coming as he half turned and shouted Help but knew they wouldn't hear but may see him mouthing the words. The truck suddenly stopped and then reversed. A woman got out and stepped before him and stood with mouth agape at the sight of a young boy naked and covered in black mud. Jack spoke to her and said that he had been attacked and his clothes had been stolen and he had been tied to the billboard but had fallen into the ditch while trying to escape.

The woman went to the truck and brought back a blanket to drape around him. Then she lowered the tailgate and helped Jack shuffle over and roll onto the back saying he was too muddy to let into the car but that it wasn't far to her house.

The truck drove to the rear of the house and Jack shuffled off the truck as she drew out a hose pipe and took the blanket away from him. After apologising for leaving him naked once more she turned the water on and a cold blast washed the mud away. When most of the mud had gone she brought a knife and cut off the rope from his ankles but said that she hadn't got anything that would cut the chain but in the meantime he would have a hot bath. She led him to the bathroom and started to fill the bath. She told him to get in the bath and then soaped him down and gave him a thorough wash and once more apologised as she dried him with a towel and had to dry his private parts. After draping a sheet around him he was taken down to the kitchen and given a meal which was hand fed to him and then put to bed. She told him her name was Janet and she was going to ring the Police about the incident and that he was to rest and try not to move and later she would try and wrap the chain in some bandages. Jack fell into a fitful slumber and was awoken when Janet came into the room with a tray of food and a bandage. She fed him some supper and then started on wrapping the chain the best she could but it meant pulling the chain where it had dug deep into Jacks flesh and then trying to force the bandage round and round. When most of the chain had at least one covering she took some cream from a tube and with her fingers tried to massage some into the sores. When she had creamed his top she threw back the bed sheets and did his ankles but leaving him naked on the bed. After the ankles she continued up his legs until suddenly grasped his genitals and began to massage them. Jack gave a gasp as he felt himself rising to efforts of Janet. He became of a heavy weight across him and saw that Janet was the weight and that she was now naked. Jack was helpless and lay there surprised and shocked but at the same time realised that this is what he had wanted with the girls. When Janet had finished she smiled at Jack as she wiped him with a towel. "Just a little treat for you." Janet replaced the covers and left the room.

The next morning the Police arrived to interview Jack and get some details but he didn't know the make of van or what the faded letters were and found it hard to describe the men in the van and could only tell of the clothes that had been stolen. He told of going to the East coast where he was to meet his parents and said that he'd have to contact them to get some more money. They told him that he could come down to the police station and look at some photographs of known suspects but the chance of finding them was very small. After doing a report they left saying that they would bring some tools to get the chain off and would be back later. Janet told Jack to follow her up to her bedroom to see if she could find something for him to wear. With no men in the house and her daughter being too small that only left her clothing. Her jeans were too small and the tee shirts he couldn't get on as he was still bound. She dressed him in a pair of her knickers that could stretch and a navy-blue skirt that had an elastic waist band. A worn pair of trainers that were a little tight but would do and a pair of stretch socks and at least his lower half was covered.

The police came back in the afternoon carrying his back pack which he identified as his. They must have thrown it away as the flag would tell everyone that it was stolen. They didn't have tools with them but asked to see what tools there were in the house to which Janet replied none. Let's have a look in the basement there usually something. Reluctantly Janet opened the door to the basement and they all trooped down. On one wall were large boards and held tools of all descriptions and each one had place and a painted image of where it should be returned to but all the cutting tools were missing. The policeman told Jack to back up to the vice and he fastened the top of the lock into the vice, took a hammer and a large screwdriver and placed the screwdriver on the bass body of the lock and with one blow it broke and fell apart. Placing the tools on the bench he led Jack back up stairs and began to loosen the chain link by link. When he reached the wrists the chain had dug deep into the flesh leaving angry looking marks of red. The loop around his neck was worse and took a lot of easing off link by link. He was free but the policeman said that he should go to the hospital and get some treatment for the injuries but Jack declined as he didn't want anyone to know he'd no cash and no identity. He told them he'd go when he got some money and could buy some new clothes and they seemed satisfied and left.

Janet left him alone that night and the next morning said that she had to visit a friend leaving him alone in the house. Jack strolled outside and saw the blanket with the black mud had been thrown in with the rubbish. He retrieved it and brushed it down and most of the mud that had dried brushed away and it just need a freshening up wash to as good as new.

In the basement he eyed the board and realised that Janet must have deliberately taken the cutting tools off the boards and they were probably in the large chest. He decided it was time to leave whether he had some new clothes or not. He took a t-shirt from the closet and the blanket and wrote a note to Janet thanking her for her kindness and set off walking back to the highway keep a sharp eye out in case Janet returned. At the highway he got a lift with a family who said that they though he was a girl and they didn't usually pick up boys. He told his story and had a great laugh when he told of wearing Janet's knickers. They took him nearly forty miles and bought him a meal at a busy diner and then said they would leave him here as they were turning off and it would be easier for him to get a ride from here.

The family left and Jack was finishing his coffee when he saw a sign that read Staff Wanted Apply Within. He asked the waitress what it was for and she replied it was for waitresses as they had two girls leave within the last week. He asked if he could apply and was told they have to wear the company's uniform that consisted of a mini dress and cap. Jack stood showing off his blue skirt and asked if he would do and the waitress called over her friend and both fell about laughing. He explained to them what had happened and said that he hadn't any money and still had two months to go before he had to meet up with his parents. His waitress was named Barbara or Babs for short and Babs took him to meet the manageress where he once more told his story. The manageress took him on as casual worker and he was taken into the storeroom to where a rack of pink dresses and caps along with red trainers. She chose one and said that it was a larger size and might fit him and left him to change. He emerged to applause from the other girls and the manageress gave him to Babs to train. The afternoon was quieter than lunchtime and Babs let him take the orders and showed him what to do. Jack soon got into the swing as it was simply repartition. Babs showed him how to lay the tables and take the money to the till and get a recite. Within a week Jack was the star of the diner with customers guessing if he was a boy or girl but too afraid to ask. If they did he would put his hand under his skirt and pretend to feel around and then say definitely a boy. Customers would get a laugh and he would get a tip. At night he use a small bed that the manageress sometime use if she worked late. One night he had just gone to bed when Babs knocked softly and he let her in. After talking for a while she kissed him gently and Jack this time responded and took her into his arms. They made love very gently and not like he had with Janet. Babs stopped with until dawn.

A month passed and soon Jack had enough money to buy new clothes and move on. He handed in his uniform and said his goodbyes to all the girls and took a lift with one of the customers saying he was going to the Grand Canyon. He was dropped off along his route but couldn't get a lift. Then he had an idea and went behind a bush and changed from his jeans back into the skirt. The next car that came along stopped for him and he explained the reason for the skirt. It appeared the people didn't like picking boy's up because they were afraid of being robbed. Jack wore his skirt all the way to the Grand Canyon and on to Los Angles finally reaching the East coast with a week to spare. Now all he had to do was to find Grandma's house. He bought a map and started tramping the streets looking for the house. He knew that it was near the sea and to the north of the main town. He was dry and needed a rest and sat down on a bench studding his map when a lady sat down and asked him where he was look2ing for. He told and she invited him into her car a said that she would help. Alone with her friend the three toured the town until after two days Jack suddenly pointed to a house and cried "There it is." As they pulled up his grandmother was in the garden and was surprised to see Jack in the car. The two ladies left after saying it had brightened up their day and Jack was charming company. Two day's later his father and mother arrived and asked him if the trip had been worthwhile. He thought of Babs and replied that it had, but he'd been robbed of his money and passport and he'd have to get a new one. His dad said that he should have stopped in a hostel until Jack replied that it was in the hostel where the robbery had taken place.

CHAPTER 6

REVENGE

Bob and Alf were friends and had been for a long time. Bob lived in his mothers flat on the top of a modest tower block. Mother doted on her son and gave him more or less what he wanted. His mother owned the rest of the block having inherited it from her husband who very conveniently for her managed to drive into a very large tramcar after imbibing an ambitious amount of alcohol. His savings and a very large insurance policy made her well off or a least comfortably off. Her days were spent dabbling in politics with an ambition to eventually be adopted as a prospective member of parliament and have the initials MP after her name. Bob had been warned on more than one occasion not to do anything to ruin her chances.

Alf was the product of a broken home. With his father away serving in the army and his mother taking a layabout as her boyfriend they divorced When Alf was very young. His mother was always at work or in the pub with her boyfriend spending the little money that they had and then the boy friend would sleep all day and beat Alf if he was woken up or had any excuse to punch the boy. Alf had to get out of the house and then was left to his own devices for far too long and had grown a little too wild. His slim build seemed to invite trouble from youths who thought that he would be an easy target to have a bit of fun with, but they soon found out that he was a wildcat in sheep's clothing. After numerous battles in the town centre where some involved the police his mother had had enough and threw him out of the house. He was given a very old small house consisting of a kitchen and a bedroom up stairs. The bedroom had at some time been divided to add a small bath and toilet. Alf had been warned by the council that if there was any more bother from him then he would be out on the street. He eventually got a job on the railway which kept him busy for a while but quit that because of the long hours, the poor pay and a general lack of interest. The only other thing he showed any talent for was football. He used to play for a local team in a local league. Bob too liked football and was a useful left back. On the field Alf became the person he was capable of being. He had skill, good football knowledge in supported his team mates and would battle his heart out for the team. Bob was running his own little business supported by his mother's money. He was a photographer and owned a little shop taking portrait pictures and children but his passion was to get away onto the moors and take landscape pictures or sporting pictures but at that time there wasn't the call for them so it was back to the humdrum job waiting for a chance to break away and do something different. Against his mothers wishes he had dropped out of school because he was bored. His mother had set him up with the photography business to give him something to do and although Bob had managed to pay his way in the shop he was still bored and restless.

Their football club was in one of the leagues out of the football leagues as such and used to play local teams mad up of older men who played for a hobby and young boys who hoped to be seen by a talent scout and move up to the main stream of football. The team did have one business sponsor who had provided a field and goal posts along with a clubhouse and changing room equipped with showers. The shower room was only small with two showers attached to a long room with lockers and two long benches, a blackboard on an easel and a desk. A large couch at the rear served as a treatment table and a kit basket held everything else.

After a particularly hard march on a muddy wet pitch where they had just lost by the odd goal the dressing room was quiet before the manager gave his usual talk to lift the boys up. Both Bob and Alf were wanting to get away to the pub but had to listen for another fifteen minutes before being able strip and head for the showers. As normal, boys would share a shower with their mates to speed up if they were heading to the pub together. A tolerant landlord would turn a blind eye and let them have a drink although he knew that it was a local football team and therefore they were not of an age to be drinking. Bob and Alf shared the shower and were soon heading to the local discussing where the team went wrong. Alf finished his drink and said that as he was unemployed and short of cash then one was all he could afford and he wasn't looking for a handout. The dole for a sixteen year old was only six shillings per week. Bob, who was a year older than Alf, smiled and said he'd buy one as payment for his company. After that the two went out together and became great friends.

Christmas neared and club was thinking of ways to raise funds and a fancy dress party were proposed and in the absence of any other ideas it was adopted. A small local hall was hired and tickets printed. Various raffle prizes were given with the proceeds going to the club funds. The only thing left to do was to decide who to go as and where to get the costumes. Back in late forty to fifties there were no shops hiring out costumes and material was still very scarce or on ration. Bob had a great idea. Before the war his mother used to have parties at her home and all the costumes would never have been thrown away but stored away somewhere in the house, in a cupboard or the attic or the garage he didn't know where and so set off to see his busy mum. Bob's mum was as usual getting ready to go to another meeting in the town when Bob arrived. Yes, she did have a few costumes somewhere around the place but hadn't seen them for a long time and didn't have the time to search for them just now. Bob was frustrated at not being able to get his hands on them right away but knew better than try to hurry her when she was going to a meeting. He was told to come back on the Monday when they would have time to go searching. Bob thought it a bit strange going to a meeting on a Sunday but said nothing.

On the Monday morning he called in as instructed to find his mother in a joyous mood. She told him that the meeting was to adopt a candidate for the local council elections and that she had won the nomination for the West Ward. The West Ward was considered a safe seat and so his mother would be a councillor. It was a good start on the political ladder. Bob had to bring her attention as to why he was here and they set off on the search starting with the large double garage but found just a pile of junk. After searching the whole house there was only one place left that they could be and that was the dusty attic. A narrow staircase ran up to the door of the attic but the door was locked and his mother had forgotten where the key was. Another search this time for the key and finally the door was unlocked and they entered the attic. A large pile of old furniture consisting of a table and three chairs, a bookcase complete with books that his mother started to read, a broken rocking horse and four old trunks. His mother put down the book and pointed to one of the trunks without say a word. Bob unfastened the rusty clasp and threw back the lid. The first that Bob noticed was a smell of mould. He picked up the first costume and it promptly fell apart in his hand as did the first few on the top of the pile. All of the costumes were made from flimsy cheap material and hadn't lasted the years that they had lain stored away. "Oh," was all his mother could say as he showed her the pile of garments. The chest was emptied but not one of the costumes could be saved.

"Can you take them to the tip for me I want to clear the attic and make an office for my work? Can you take the cupboards as well? I've got some new stuff coming after we've decorated and having some heating put in. There are some clothes from our old drama group but I'm afraid they're all for ladies."

Bob opened one of the wardrobes and it held about a dozen different costumes of the twenty to thirties era. The wardrobe had a top shelf and a drawer below. The shelf was stuffed with handbags and hats or headbands and lots of costume jewels. He checked the drawer and found several pairs of shoes and the more bob thought about it the more an idea formed in his mind. They could turn the fancy dress party into a thirties themed party. There was enough for all the boys to go as flappers and if everybody was dress up it wouldn't be an embarrassment to anyone. He rushed downstairs to the telephone and rang the football club. After talking for five minutes he put down the phone and waited. Soon a van pulled up and out trooped most of the football team. Bob led them to the attic and ten minutes later the attic was clear, the team had their costumes, and the club had loads of furniture to sell for their funds, but not before Bob had chosen two of the best costumes for himself and Alf. The first costume was a red flapper dress with a white diamante headband sporting a red feather. Red shoes and a small bag with a red cord to go over the shoulder completed the outfit. The second costume was that of a French Maid. This costume looked as though it was made of black silk although bob thought it unlikely to be silk. It had a very short skirt with a little white apron and frilly white underwear that would show as soon as the wearer moved. More white frills were on the bust line and a small cap with two ribbons hanging from it completed the outfit. One pair of red and a pair of black shoes along with nylons was needed for both boys and his mother would be able to get those.

Things changed a little. Another week had passed and the dance was now going to be a disco at Christmas and another dance at the New Year was to be the fancy dress. This was to get two lots of revenue from the same idea and it would give more time to get the costumes right. Mother suddenly handed him a bag that contained one pair of black and one pair of red shoes and two pair of nylons. This surprised bob a little as usually she hadn't the time to think of bob's needs without him having to remind her several times. He found out a week later when she announced that the block where bob's shop was located had been sold for redevelopment and that included the shop. The one he thought was his was apparently not his as the deeds hadn't been changed to his name. Now he was out of business and a job but as his mother said he was a bit young to be in business and now he could be her campaign manager for the election for although it was considered a safe seat she wasn't taking any chances.

All the large props in the shop were moved into his mother's garage and the small stuff and his cameras into his flat where he built a small darkroom tacked onto the kitchen. The flat was in a different block also owned by his mother but she said that this block wasn't going to be sold so his flat was safe. As it was still two weeks before Christmas and there wasn't a lot to do as a campaign manager because the elections were in May. Bob told Alf to call at the flat on the Saturday so that they could try on their costumes and his mother would bring some make up and then be able to see if the dresses needed any alteration. Alf arrived just after lunch and the boys unpacked the dresses. They stripped and each wore a pair of trunks before putting on the underwear. Alf was a little smaller than bob and his flapper dress dropped neatly over his shoulders but bob was having a struggle with the maids outfit and had to pull it down but even then it was tight and he hardly dared to move just in case it split the material. Just then his mother arrived with the makeup. "That's no good, it's far too tight." She said circling bob.

"Can't you alter it?" Bob asked.

"No, the costume was especially made and it has three layers and padding in between the layers. We were doing a murder play and I remember the vicar did it. Janet played the maid and we didn't have a maid outfit and Mrs Smith volunteered to make one and there was a row when she brought it in because instead of an ordinary maids outfit she had made a French maids one. We argued whether to use it or not but we needed a maid in the plot and there wasn't any more time to make another so it had to do. Still the men liked it. I've an idea, you can swap with Alf he's a little smaller than you so it should fit him." Bob didn't like the idea of losing the maid outfit as nearly all of the other boys would be flappers and there was only one maid costume but it appeared that he'd no choice as his mother couldn't alter it. He pulled the costume off and picked up the flapper dress. Alf slipped the maids costume over his shoulder and it slipped easily down as though it had been made for him.

"There, that's much better," remarked Bob's mum as she circled Alf. "But your going to stretch it putting it on that way, it's got fasteners down the back." Alf reach around the back of his costume and could feel the little bumps all the way down. "They're called hook and eye fasteners and if you loosen them the dress will simply drop down. Now where's the box with all the underclothes?" Alf brought the box that had contained the clothes and also the shoe box with the shoes and nylons. After sorting through all the garments she made two piles of clothing, one for the maid and the other for the flapper costume.

"It's a pity that I couldn't get any black nylons as a maid would wear but they are very scarce so these will have to do."

She made Alf remove the costume and put on the nylons after showing him how. This was followed by a white slip and a white girdle leaving Alf with a slightly embarrassed look upon his face. It was then that she found that the bras were missing. After measuring his chest and that of Bobs she stated that it was a good job she had come as boys were hopeless at dressing. Bob was going to point out that they didn't usually put on nylons and bras and then decided to keep quiet as his mother got out the makeup. Soon Alf had eye shadow and lipstick and a little powder on his face. The costume was place around him and the hooks and eyes done up. The maids cap was pinned onto his head and with a little padding instead of the bra he was done.

He had to walk up and down the flat and in spite of the high heels he appeared to have no difficulty. He stopped in front of the half length mirror which was the longest mirror in the place, and admired his image and concluded that if it wasn't for his short hair then he would have difficulty telling if he was a boy or a girl. Bob's mum also seemed pleased. "There I told you, he makes a smashing girl. I think I'll hire him as a maid for the house." Bob smiled at her remark as he knew that it was her attempt at humour, or at least he hoped it was humour but the more that he watched Alf walking up and down the more he suspected his mother would carryout her threat.

"What about me, don't I need something?"

"No just the padded bra and a bit of make up and then you'll do." Bob felt a little let down. True to her word the padded bras were delivered and the only thing to do was to practice putting on the make up. At the end of the second week the club had the Christmas party and Bob's mother invited Alf around to share their Christmas dinner. Bob gave Alf a bottle of wine to give to his mum as he knew that Alf would be broke as usual and then in the evening the two boys went to their local pub to spend the night. One week later and it was New Year's Eve and time for the fancy dress party. The costumes were stored at bob's flat and Alf arrived in good time to change before Bob's mum came to pick them up in the car and take them to the club. They stripped and put on the trunks and then the rest of the underclothes including the padded bras. They helped each other with the hook and eyes on the dresses and then started on the nail polish and eye makeup. They were nearly ready as Bobs mum made her entrance and condemned their efforts with the makeup and wiped it off and redid it. After the lipstick and a little powder she did Bobs and then placed Bob's diamantine headband and red feather on his head and Alf's little cap with the black ribbons. She then stood back and after inspecting them both gave a little nod of approval. "Don't forget that I'll not be able to pick you up and you'll have to get a taxi or a lift and at New Year it'll be expensive. You'd better take this just in case." Bob was given enough money to be able to get back home and enough for drinks as well. After a final inspection she ushered them out to the car and off to the party.

The party was a great success with dancing and a quiz for a small cash prize, some free drinks and then a parade of all the fancy dress costumes for a prize of a crate of beer. Each person had to parade down the length of the hall and at the end the judges voted that the winner was Alf in his French Maid outfit. After singing the traditional Auld Lang

Sine some of the boys and their girl friends started dancing and Bob took Alf in his arms and finished the dance, and then it was time to go home. They were fortunate to get a lift back to Bob's place that not only saved them the taxi fare but got them home quickly as Alf was nearly asleep. Bob half carried Alf up to the flat and then came back for the crate of beer which was placed in the kitchen. He then took a bowl of hot water and placed it in front of the fire. Picking Alf up he started to undress him taking off the dress and underclothes. He made him stand in the bowl of water and then proceeded to wash him down with a warm soapy flannel. After each part of his body was washed Bob would give it a little kiss until Alf was beginning to respond to the kisses. When reaching his groin Bob suddenly kissed Alf's genitals and started giving him oral sex until he responded. Bob lifted him out of the water and sat him on the edge of the bed and dried his feet and then laid Alf down in the bed. Bob had a quick wash and joined Alf in the bed snuggling up and holding him in his arms and although Alf was already dropping of to sleep Bob once again started kissing him until he finally turned him onto his stomach and wrapped an arm under him pulling him into a kneeling position. Alf awoke with a pain at his rear. Bob with the help of a jar of Vaseline had penetrated him. Alf tried to pull away but Bob held him tight until he had finished and released him.

Bob turned Alf towards him telling him that he loved him and let Alf fall asleep in his arms.

Alf was very quiet the next morning as it had been a bit of a shock when Bob had shagged him. He dressed and left the flat and didn't respond to Bob's call of "See you at the match."

He thought that things had gone too far and wondered how to get out of it. The match was the first one of the of the season after the Christmas break and the team were in the middle of the table which wasn't bad as it was a new team in a higher division. Things got better when he received a letter to inform him that he'd got a job with the Post Office as a telegraph boy delivering telegrams using a small BSA red motor bike and to start the next Monday. Bob was also busy as the council elections were in two months and there were leaflets to write and print and all the volunteers to organise the deliveries. Two months later came the elections and as expected Bob's mother won her safe seat with an increased majority as she was well known in the district for her charity work. A party for the volunteer workers was organised and then Bob's work would be finished. The council leader came to congratulate everyone and invite the top officials to a fundraising event for all the business men who had supported the party. This would be a full sit down lunch and a raffle of donated gifts with the proceeds to party funds. After a short spell of dancing the main event would start with speeches and then an auction of donated gifts. These gifts would be special ones of things that could not be bought such as tickets for special football matches or race courses and holidays aboard. Among those attending would be the business man who ran the football team that both Bob and Alf played for. He had the idea to have six of the boys attend in their costumes to sell the tickets which everyone thought was a great idea without asking the boys.

One Sunday evening in June the boys were in Bob's flat changing into their dresses to go to the venue, and waiting for their car. It was the first time they got the chance to talk together for a while after what had happened. Bob asked why Alf had stopped coming and when Alf mentioned the rape Bob said that he was sorry and it was only because he loved Alf. After talking for a while Alf said that he would come the next Saturday. Just then the car arrived and they hadn't any more time to talk. The occasion was a great success and it was after one pm before they got back to the flat. Bob's mother waited until Alf had changed out of his costume and then ran him home.

Alf loved his new job at the Post Office. He had new mates and he loved riding the motorcycle delivering the telegrams. Saturday came around and he decided not to go to Bobs as he had promised but to go out with a couple of his new friends. Another week passed and when it was the Saturday again he was awakened by a banging on his front door. He looked out of the window to see Bob outside pointing at something pinned up on a telephone pole outside. After quickly dressing he went out and found that it was a photograph of himself completely in the nude and worse was that there was another photograph a few yards away. He looked around and in the distance was another but this time it was a picture of him standing in the bra and knickers wearing the girdle. All the way to bobs flat were pictures of Alf in various poses pinned up for all to see. He looked at his watch and saw that it was just after five in the morning. At least he thought that he get them all down before they were seen by the workers going to work.

Alf arrived to find Bob waiting for him calmly making a cup of tea. Alf demanded to know that he was doing by pinning up the pictures and didn't he know that he could be fired from his new job for such a stunt. Bob just said that he had promised to come and had broken his promise. Alf looked at the sheaf of pictures and said that if Bob would give him the pictures and the negatives then he would come back. Bob thought about the offer and said that he would but he wanted something that Alf valued in place of the snaps. Alf said that he hadn't anything but Bob said his grandfathers pocket watch and his photos of his grandmother and a dog that they once had and various bits that made the total to ten. Alf knew that he was trapped but desperately wanted the pictures of himself in the nude, so that he could destroy them. He had a guarantee from Bob that these were the only pictures and negatives that existed and therefore agreed. He set off to back home to collect the articles to exchange. Shortly afterwards he returned and Bob checked the contents of the box. When satisfied he placed the box in his safe and gave Alf a letter that said Alf agreed to come and stay with bob every Saturday and obey his instructions and be his maid. If he broke his promise then Bob had the right to destroy one of the articles that were in Alf's box and to do so every time that he disobeyed. He asked Alf to sign the letter and although Alf wasn't happy he did sign. Bob placed the letter inside his safe and handed over the incriminating negatives to Alf who promptly set fire to them on the gas stove.

"I'll call you Missy and you can call me Master," said Bob. "Now get changed and then you can make us breakfast."

"I'm not calling you master I only agreed to come here on a Saturday." Bob handed over a copy of the letter that Alf had just signed. "The letter says you will obey my instructions and you signed it." Bob waited until Alf had finished reading it. "I thought it meant to just be a maid." "Well it doesn't so get stripped Missy. Alf had been in too much of a hurry and had not read the letter as thoroughly as he ought and now had agreed to be Bob's plaything. It was too late to do anything for the moment and he needed time to think. He reluctantly went to the big chest where the maids costume was kept and started to strip. Alf had nearly finished dressing when he had only the shoes and knickers to put on.

"Let's see if you have learned your lesson," said Bob. "Come here and bend over. Bob was taking off his belt. Alf couldn't believe that he would go so far and was about to refuse and then thought that would play right into his hands as he had been given an instruction and Bob could destroy something from his box. He walked to the settee and bent over the arm. Bob pushed the short skirt up over his back and the first stinging blow fell onto Alf's bare buttocks to be followed by five more. When finished bob lifted Alf up and gave him a kiss saying that now all the unpleasantness was over. Alf picked up his maids knickers and walked slowly to the kitchen.

The football season was in full swing again and a few new players arrived. The players in the teams they were playing were larger that those they were used to play against and injuries were frequent and the team could be different from week to week. Bob's mother settled into her role as a councillor and appeared to enjoy the role but that left Bob with very little to do except to pursue his hobby out on the hills with his camera, but that didn't earn him a living. Alf was at his work all week and didn't see Bob until he turned up on the Saturday to be Bobs maid and then at football on the Sunday. The football season ended at the end of April but Bob still insisted that Alf had to report for his duty as a maid. His duty now included cleaning all of the flat and also doing Bob's washing by hand of his underwear and if it wasn't done to Bob's satisfaction he would be made to bend over the arm of the settee and take another beating. At the weekend he reported at Bob's place as usual and changed into his costume. After cooking and serving bob's breakfast he asked if Bob would type him a letter as they knew that Alf would soon have to report for National Service and serve two years in the forces but instead of Alf waiting until they called him up he'd like to go in now. He would also like to join one of the Scottish regiments. Bob who had managed to get a deferment for his National Service was a little surprised but agreed. A person in a reserved occupation could put off going until his apprenticeship had finished and his mum had got one for Bob. He asked what the address of Alf's flat was but Alf said that he was giving up the flat and could the letter be addressed to Bobs place as he would be here every week. Bob agreed and typed the letter finally pulling it from the typewriter and handing it to Alf saying he shouldn't forget to sign it. Alf read it and then folded it up and placed it on the chest where his clothes were.

The next week as Alf was changing to return back to his flat, Bob asked Alf if he would write to him when he enlisted but Alf said no, as he couldn't forget the rape and that it had upset him. Bob thought about it and said that they would only have a few more Saturdays together and he didn't want to part on bad terms. The only thing to do was to try and make up the damage caused for one stupid act. The next week he would change places and be the maid. He would wear the dress and obey every command that Alf would give him, to clean his flat and make his breakfast. Alf could use him just the same as he did on that night and beat and rape him and for him to take his revenge.

"That's not good enough. I have had to be your slave for weeks and I want the weeks until I go for National Service," said Alf. "But that could be more that a month" Bob answered. "Then I'm going," replied Alf, and made for the door. Bob shouted "No I agree." Alf turned around. "I want your word and as a safeguard of all the contents to your safe if you don't obey me." Bob nodded his consent. "I also want to keep the key of the safe to stop you from getting in if you disobey." Bob knew that there was about a hundred pounds in the safe that was a lot of money in those days but thought that he could manage for three Saturday's so he agreed. Alf gave Bob a piece of paper on which he made Bob type the words the words; I promise to obey Alf for the weeks until he reports for Nation Service in the forces and do everything he orders me to do and also to agree to give him the contents of the safe and my safe key and my goods being destroyed if I refuse to carry out his orders. He read through the document and realised what power it gave to Alf but at the same time was desperate to make amends for his one act of madness.

He reluctantly reached for his pen and signed handing the paper to Alf who looked at the signature and then folded the paper and put it into his pocket. Next he held out his hand for the key. Bob reached into his pocket and pulled out the safe key handing it to Alf. "Mum has the spare key," he said. Alf took the key and the signed paper and left the flat. He had things to do. The next week Alf turned up at Bob's flat as usual and was welcomed inside.

"Alright Missy, said Alf. Let's see if you are as good as your word, get stripped." Bob obediently started to undress until Alf shouted to him to hurry. Alf opened the chest with the maids outfit and threw out the bra and the girdle with the slip and waited until Bob had adjusted the straps and then put them on. The black dress was next but even with all the hook and eyes being loosened it was a tight fit and the top two had to be left loose.

He finished off with the stockings and shoes which pinched a little bit and then reached for the knickers and the pair of trunks to wear underneath.

"Leave them and come here and bend over for taking much too long." Bob hadn't expected to be punished and very nearly said no but remembered it was one of the last times and so after muttering "Yes Master," he bent over the end of the settee as Alf took off his belt and thought back to the time when he had been beaten. The first blow fell with such a force that made Bob wince. Alf took his time over the remaining strokes until Bob's rear end was red and smarting with pain. He was going to give it a rub when Alf told him to leave it alone and let it smart. Alf's next order was to Missy to open the safe and bring out my box. Missy obeyed and gave up the box and his hold on Alf as the key was handed back and dropped into Alf's pocket.

"Right, said Alf. "We are going to my place where you have work to do so go and fix your make up" Bob didn't reply but gave a little start as he hadn't expected to leave his flat and was thinking about cleaning his flat not Alf's. "Are you ready yet?" Bob came out in full make up and began heading for the door until Alf suddenly remembered and called out to bring his camera and plenty of film. Bob returned to the darkroom and picked up his camera and a spare reel of film. He handed the camera to Alf who checked that there was film and a spare reel and then headed for the door followed by a sheepish looking Bob who would be wearing the very short maids costume in public as by now the streets were getting a little bit busier. He had done the make up as best as he could and as Alf walked to the door he reached for his knickers to cover his still red rear. "Leave them, you don't need them do you." Bob felt the cold wind through the flimsy material as they walked out of the flat, and Alf took the key and locked the door just in case Bob got cold feet and tried to go back. They set off down the road and Alf told Missy not to hold down the skirt leaving bob distinctly embarrassed. The shoes were pinching, the skirt was too short especially as he'd only the knickers underneath and at the party they wore a pair of trunks but they were back in the flat and the wind was very cold. The few people that were about gave them a strange look as the pair made their way to the flat. On the way down they passed a local Fish and Chip shop that would be open at lunch time for the football crowds who could get a meal after being in the pub and then going to the match. Alf's flat was just at the bottom of the street in a little courtyard made up from four houses set in a square. At one time the houses would have been shared homes with two or more families sharing the four outside toilets but the toilets had been left unused when the upstairs bedroom was divided off to make a tiny bathroom and a bedroom with the kitchen/diner room below and the houses being turned into one family homes. The two houses opposite the one occupied by Alf were not in use and were boarded up.

When they finally reached the flat Missy nearly ran inside to be met with what could only be described as a tip.

When Alf had got the agreement with Bob he started planning what to do. His flat needed cleaning and that would do for a start as he hardly ever cleaned it, but just to make sure it needed more dirt. The dustbins in the yard were galvanised tubs to enable the people to place hot ashes inside without the ashes setting fire to anything. Alf picked up the little shovel and went to his neighbours bin and scooped a shovelful of ash which then was sprinkled all over the square of carpet. Next was the toilet. Hanging from a piece of string were squares of torn up newspapers that served as toilet paper. He took half a dozen of the squares and rolled them up into little balls and rammed them down the pan until they compacted into a solid mass. A pull of the chain saw the pan half flood before the water went down. He screwed a few more newspaper balls and placed them into the pan just to make sure that the toilet would be well and truly blocked. The gas meter was checked. He found it was well stocked with shillings meaning plenty of gas that would last over a week. Alf turned on all the gas taps and let each one burn. The next morning there was only enough gas for about two days. He next contacted the council to ask them to take away all the furniture as he was being called up and was given a date when it was to be collected. With all his plans in place except one he settled down and two day's later on the Saturday set off to bob's flat.

Missy's feet nearly sank into the carpet from all the mess. Cinders crunched under his feet and dust clouds rose from the floor that hadn't been swept for ages. "How can anyone live in a place like this," exclaimed Bob.

"Well your mum rents out places like this. Alf replied.

"No she doesn't, not as bad as this, Bob replied. Alf had laid a trap and Bob was falling right into it.

"Would you live in any flat owned by your mother and rented out? Alf asked.

"Of course I would, any at all." "Right then, that's settled." You can move in immediately. "What do you mean move in." "This is my flat and it is owned by your mother and you said that you could live in any flat owned by your mother so you are going to get your chance. You can live here and I'll move into your flat." Bob had a look of amazement his face. "My mother owns this flat?" "Yes," said Alf. "She rents it out to the council and they use it for emergency accommodation and gave it to me and now you've got it." Alf had left some cleaning materials and a bucket of water along with a small hand brush and a bar of soap.

"I want the flat cleaned from top to bottom and when you're finished with this room there's the upstairs. And I don't want you getting the dress dirty so you'd better take it off." Bob began to strip. "What shall I wear, I'll have to go outside to empty out the dirty water." "I'll get you something, replied Alf as he walked out of the flat to put the next phase of his plan into action. He returned to Bob's flat and packed up the maids dress and took it down to the football club where he said Bob and himself are resigning because of being called up. Next he went to bob's mum and told him that Bob had gone away on holiday before his call up and would she see to clearing the flat and selling it as he would be in the army for two years and Alf would stay in the flat until bob's things had been removed. On his way he passed a second hand shop that had a floral dress in the window and an idea formed in his mind. It was only 5 shillings and another 2 shillings for a pair of sandals. Once in Bob's flat he found a pair of underpants that would do. The dress was a long one that was the fashion before the war. He took the kitchen scissors' and sliced of a good eighteen inches from the bottom of the dress and then took it down to Bob. The dress was nearly as short as the maids dress being a good six inches above the knee but now he had the underpants underneath. The carpet was still a mess and Alf told him to roll it up and throw it outside along with the two old bed sheets and the curtains. Between them they stripped the flat of all the furniture and contents and then Alf said that he wanted Bob to do a little posing for him. Alf took out the camera and had bob move to various positions and then told him to strip naked and do them all over again.

"I'll want these developing tonight at about eleven so don't go to bed."

Alf called back at 11pm and told Bob to dress. A chill wind made Bob shiver as he stepped out of the flat although it was only the end of August. His shortened summer dress offered very little in the way of warmth and not having any stockings didn't help. Thankfully the streets were very quiet as all the pubs had closed at ten and the last drinkers had gone home to their beds. Bob set about developing the photo's into six by eight inches until he had twenty and that was enough. Alf started looking through the drawers in the flat watched by bob as it was all belonging to him. In one of the drawers he found a bottle of strong paste. Just the thing I need he thought.

"Right lets go. Would you like some chips for supper?" Bob said he would like the chips, but go where as it after midnight and so Saturday was over. Alf gave a little smile and handed a copy of the agreement to bob.

"The agreement doesn't say three Saturdays but the weeks until I join up." Bob read though the agreement three times but no matter how he read it meant all the weeks and he hadn't seen the difference and now he'd signed it. "But I meant the three Saturdays not weeks." He protested.

"You know what you told me, you should not sign until you understand just what you're signing and now you're stuck with it so let's go."

They arrived at the top of the little street leading to Alf's flat. The chip shop was closed with no one in sight but all around was evidence that the shop had been open as chip papers were strewn all around.

"Pick up all the chip papers and well put them in the waste bin." Bob started collecting the screwed up papers and Alf opened them out until he gave a little shout of triumph and held up one still containing chips that somebody had half eaten and thrown the rest away. "Look you've got your supper." "What do you mean," asked Bob." Well you can buy some if you've got enough money but I'm not giving you any and this is every day so you'd better start saving food whenever you get the chance," replied Alf.

They collected three more papers containing chips and took them down to the flat. "I don't want you dirtying your dress so you'd better let me have it.

Bob was freezing cold but had to remove the thin dress and then Alf nodded towards the underpants and he had to remove them along with the sandals. He was naked and Alf wrapped the garments in a spare but clean chip paper and told Bob to carry on cleaning the floor and when it grew light enough to see, then he could paste the pictures over the windows as from now on this was to be his new home. Alf slammed the door shut and turned the big key locking bob in the flat, cold, and naked with just some greasy old chip to eat.

Bob spent all of Sunday working on the floor and the windows as it was the only way to try and keep warm. In the meantime he was trying to think of how to get out of the agreement. His mother's solicitor could probable get him out of it if they went to court but the publicity would finish her ambition as a politician. For the moment he was stuck with it and Alf knew it.

Alf arrived bright and early the next day and threw the dress to Bob. The council are coming this morning to clear the flat so we must have everything out of here by then. The bed was thrown out and all the kitchen crockery and the table. The contents of the cupboards and the curtain pole were piled on the top until the only thing left was a small scrub brush and a block of carbolic soap and a bucket of water. When they had finished the wagon arrived and took all the stuff away to the local dump as it was all too old to be used again. Alf told the man in charge that the key would be returned when he had cleaned the place and to give him five weeks as the rent was paid until then. "Get this floor scrubbed and when you've done that clear the blocked toilet. I'll be back later." Bob had been expecting to go back to his own flat to clean but it appeared that Alf had other ideas. "Can't I stay in my flat as it's too cold here" Alf ignored him.

At five pm he returned and shouted to Bob to hurry as they were going out. Bob dressed once again and stepped out hurrying after Alf who went up into the town to an open air market. Underneath some of the stalls some rotten fruit had been thrown and left for the cleaners. Alf pointed at the fruit and said one word "Fetch" Bob found a carrier bag and dived under collecting rotten apples and oranges along with rotting potatoes and squashed berries. And cabbage leaves. Fifteen minutes later he was back in the empty flat standing naked and listening to the door being slammed and the key turning in the lock as Alf left. It grew dark and as it did the colder it got. Bob was going to peel the potatoes when he remembered that he didn't have a peeler or a knife. He placed the bag by the fireside and started to sort the fruit when suddenly there was a plop sound and the gas fire went out. He checked the meter and saw that it was empty and worse was to follow as the lights went out as the electric went off. It grew dark and now he couldn't see what to eat as the square wasn't lit. Without the gas it was cold and he was trying to think how to get warm but he didn't even have a bed. He curled up on the floor quietly sobbing and shivering.

Alf was as good as his word and returned after dark. The noise of the key turning in the lock aroused Bob as he was curled up on the floor cold and stiff. Alf couldn't see him on the floor but threw in the dress and told him to dress and come out. The sound of someone stirring meant that bob had heard and in two minutes he stretched his tired aching muscles and followed Alf up the street not bothered who may see them.

The flat was nice and warm and Bob wanted to know if he could have a bath but was refused.

"You're not here for that you're here to write a letter to your mum now get a pen and write what I say." Dear mum, I'm sorry that I've let you down again. It's true that I've had a homosexual affair and attacked Alf who didn't give his permission. I've also sent nude pictures of myself to a well known magazine. I'm going away so I don't embarrass you again and in a year or two, I may come back and beg your forgiveness. Bob.

"I haven't sent any pictures to a magazine."

"No, I sent them on your behalf, now write it down and sign it." Bob wrote it down and then added his signature and handed it to Alf.

"Now get some hot water and scrub my floor and later well go scavenging." Two hour passed with bob now nice and warm but working hard as Alf demanded the flat be cleaned from top to bottom. When finished it was time to go and Bob looked longingly at his fridge and the coffee on the kitchen table but wasn't offered any. He'd been working for almost three hours and was feeling tired but Alf opened the door and told him to come out.

The town was quiet and they wandered up and down the streets looking for anything to eat. A half loaf of stale bread was all they could find as there hadn't been a market and their local chippy was closed. The local bakers used outside bins for the unsold products and were full of bread and cakes but also the bins were swarming with cockroaches. The roaches were attracted to the warmth of the ovens and the easy supply of food.

"Well at least you've got supper," said Alf. Bob stared at the cockroaches and the food. "There could be some good stuff underneath." The roaches had scattered with the lifting of the lid of the bin and now bob began moving the top layer of buns to get at what was underneath choosing those without jam or sugar hoping that they were the cleaner of what was there. Bob wrapped the buns in paper to take them back to the flat.

Next morning Alf took the letter now sealed in an envelope over to the town hall and handed it over to Bob's mum. She didn't say anything but he could see she was visually shocked and demanded to see for herself. Alf thought that she meant immediately, but then she said after lunch, and as it was nearly one pm it gave him an hour to get bob out. He couldn't march through the town as Bob could be recognised but he may have an idea and hurried down to the flat. Bob was surprised as the door opened but was in a panic when told his mother was on her way down.

"The lavatory, it's the only place." Alf pointed across the little square to the unused toilets. "Take everything out." The water bucket and soap and flannel were grabbed and what was left of the bread and buns were carried over to the toilets and one of the doors was forced open. Bob sat on the toilet pan with all the goods around him and waited as Alf did a final check only to notice the toilet upstairs was still blocked. At two a car drew up and out got Bob's mum with another man. Alf was waiting and did a conducted tour of the flat. They noticed the poor condition of the place and understood that was why Alf had taken temporary possession of bobs place as this place wasn't fit to be lived in. As they descended from the bedroom they spotted bobs pictures glued to the windows. "The filthy little devil he wasn't brought up to behave like that; he used to be such a good boy." Bob's mum muttered as she opened the car door. Alf stepped in. I'm using bobs flat but I'll leave as soon as this ones ready as the rent is paid for another three weeks and then I'll soon be called up for my National Service. "Stay as long as you want as this place needs pulling down but can you get the pictures off before you go?" Bob's mum asked. "You can rely on me and nobody will ever know from me what went on here," replied Alf. "Can you do me a favour? I'm having a bit of trouble sleeping but my Doctor doesn't want me having sleeping tablets as he thinks I'll do something silly. And we need some indelible ink to mark the team's kit as the numbers keep washing off, do you know where we can get a small bottle?" "I think we can manage that and I'll send a man to the flat to see what we can sell." Bob's mum put the car into gear grateful that Alf can be relied upon when Alf told her that there were bob's private papers in the safe and also a lot of money. "I'll call in the morning." She let out the clutch and the car drove away.

Bob's mum arrived at ten am. Alf showed her into the flat which had been cleaned by Missy and commented on how clean it was and Alf was doing a good job. She handed him a little parcel containing some sleeping powders and a bottle of inedible ink. "These are from my doctor and they are full strength so do take care as one will do for about four hours." Alf thanked her and offered to pay for them but she wouldn't take any money from him. "Just look after the place for me while I get a sale and then it'll take about six weeks before it goes through. No need to pay me any rent just cover any bills, now where's the safe." Alf opened the safe and took out the box containing Bob's private papers and after sorting through them she said that at least there wasn't anything there of a bad nature.

"Bob will have his army pay when he enlists so it may be as well if you cancel his allowance. Can you arrange for your man to take out the meters from the flat as someone may break in looking for money and also the water needs turning off as it is coming colder and it may freeze and we don't want a flood."

"Oh that's brilliant, I'm glad you thought of that." She picked up all of the money and then gave £5 back to Alf. "That's for being a good boy. I'll see to it and thank you and you will let me know when you have to go won't you." Alf gave a nod and Bob's mum swept out of the door.

Alf got a note to say a man would come to turn the water off and the gas and electric boards also arrived and took out the gas fire and the meters. Alf met the water man and made sure that the toilets across the yard remained on as a gentleman was still using them. The man inserted a long spanner into a hole in the pavement and turned. He entered the flat and tried turning the valve and had to bring a tool to free up the valve after Alf had turned it off. No water came from the tap and satisfied he left. Alf let Missy out of the toilet saying that all the men had gone. The flat was a mess having all the services torn out. "Look on the bright side at least you can have a wood fire now that the gas fire is missing. As soon as it gets dark fill your buckets and then come to the flat. He gave Bob the key and returned to his flat but didn't mention that his mum had taken all his money and documents from the safe.

Missy arrived. "Change into a suit and pack all your clothes into the other suitcase and take the lot down to the pawnbrokers before they close. Your mum wants everything out and the lot has to be sold before some prospective buyers turn up." Alf handed bob a pair of scissors. Cut up all the underwear that can't be sold. Missy didn't like the clothes going and was going to mention it but knew that it wouldn't make any difference and it would give him the chance to wear his suit again. Take your dress with you and leave it at the flat and then change and go scavenging. I'm back at work tomorrow and I'll collect the tickets after work and don't spend any of the money as your mum will want the cash." His mum didn't want the cash but Alf did.

In the afternoon he saw a couple of his old team-mates and stopped his motorbike to have a word. They told him they had got the notice to attend for a medical prior to their National service and another one of the team had already got his posting. Alf asked how long it took from the medical to the posting and was told about one month. That meant six week from start to finish. It was time to put plan B into action.

Bob called at the market and didn't find any food but did find a piece of sheeting that was used for roofing the stalls.

He took it back to the flat and cut out and oblong shape and then cut a circle in the centre. After putting his head through the sheeting was now a poncho, a sort of one piece rain coat. It wasn't very elegant but it would keep a lot of rain from him if Alf would let him keep it. Two weeks later Bob got a letter telling him to report for a medical which surprised him as he was on deferment unless they had found out that his business had finished. He reported as ordered and was told that he'd passed as being fit for duty. In September Alf received a letter ordering him to report for his medical and as Bob before him he was passed fit for duty. Three weeks later when bob was in the bathroom cleaning the floor the post arrived. A quick look to see if bob had heard showed him that he hadn't so Alf picked up the letter and hid it. Later that night when Bob was locked back at the house Alf opened the letter to bob. He read the news that Bob had been posted to Scotland to join a Scottish Highland Regiment based in Glasgow. Alf smiled as it was he who had put Bob's name on the letter that he had asked to be typed and now in three weeks he would have his revenge. Alf also expected a letter telling him to report but reckoned that he'd plenty of time because he wouldn't be volunteering to go in early. At the weekend Alf reported to Bob that he had to go for his medical and as he'd asked to go in early he expected to go in the next three or four weeks.

Alf had furnished the flat with a small axe and told bob to chop up the cupboards for firewood. He also gave a knife to peel and food that needed peeling. It started to rain and bob put on his new raincoat. Alf looked at it had to decide whether or not to allow it. Finally he said that it was too long and order Bob to shorten it by six inches. It was now two inches shorter that his dress. He protested that the rain would run down soaking the bottom of the dress but was told that was the idea as it was part of his punishment. Bob took the poncho off and took out his knife.

They went scavenging but the picking was slim. Over the weeks bob had grown thin but had to find his own food. All the usual places had been tried but they found nothing. Alf mentioned that there was a restaurant at the top end of the town but the rear yard was closed. Bob asked if they could try as it meant going hungry if he couldn't find something. A large gate barred the way to the rear of the premises but they could see the bins in the yard. The restaurant was closed as it was nearly eleven thirty. Bob asked permission to climb the gate and see what there was. The yard was very dark and Alf wasn't sure that he could do it without making a noise but bob pleaded Alf to let him try. Bob shinned over the gate and crept to the bins. The first two didn't have anything but the third bin was labelled Pigs. These bins were left from the war years where uneaten food was saved for the farmers to feed to their pigs so nothing was wasted. Bob felt the bin was heavy but couldn't see inside, however something was in and he got his tin out and filled the large tin with whatever was inside and made for the gate. Back in his house Alf locked the door on a now naked Bob and set off home after locking the clothing in the toilet opposite. Bob ate his fill of something gooey from the tin and tried to get to sleep although the fire had gone out and he was freezing. Alf called in before work just as it was becoming light to find bob in pain. The bin was writhing with maggots which may be unpleasant to eat but something else had been added to the food to either prevent theft or kill the maggots and bob had eaten it. After his first delivery Alf called in at the chemist before returning to the Post Office. He bought the largest bottle of Cod Liver Oil hoping to flush the poison out of his system. He unlocked the door and made Bob kneel and open his mouth while he poured half a cupful into him. Bob spluttered at the taste but Alf insisted that he take another half a cupful. Were not going there again said Alf.

Alf took bob to his flat to get warm and to give him some soup. Bob was still poorly and Alf washed him and put him to bed. Later Alf joined him and held him until he slept more easily. He had been a little frightened at Bob's collapse and vowed to be more careful.

Bob recovered and was made to return to the house. Once there he was stripped and locked in but not before Alf had made him swallow a powder saying that it would help him recover. After work he called in and Bob was up waiting for him. The next day Alf once more gave Bob a powder but a slightly larger dose. He called in again after work and Bob was still sleeping. Alf reckoned that a dose and half should be about right.

That evening Alf was making a meal when he heard someone at the door. Bob's mum had brought a dealer to appraise the cameras. After some trading mainly because Bob's mum knew the value of the goods as she had bought them when setting up the camera shop, a deal was struck and after Alf reminded her of the goods in her garage, they left. At lunchtime the next day a van arrived and took all the equipment away including the darkroom with its trays and the chemicals. Alf went back to work but called in to the house and told bob to change into his last suit and with the money raised from the pawning of the other suits he should go to the second hand Market and buy a new black dress complete with all the under garments. He gave bob a list with the sizes written down. Alf had taken the measurements from the maid's outfit that was too tight on Bob and added a size larger, and then he had to come to the flat and try on the dress. Bob was wondering why but had no alternative but to follow orders. A suitcase containing his last suit with a shirt and socks and shoes was left and Alf carried on to his work. That evening Bob arrived with all the new goods and was told to strip and put on the new dress. Alf circled him and saw that the dress was a good fit and just needed a handbag and topcoat to be complete. Bob saw that his cameras were missing and that his darkroom had been stripped. At least said Alf, it will give you some firewood.

It's time to set off. Put the suit into the case and leave the dress here. Bob did as he was told and changed back into the summer dress and then they set off to the house having pulled down a piece of the darkroom for the fire. The house was dark as usual with just a little fire. It had rained for most of the day and once again nothing could be found. The chip shop had been cleaned up and the market swept up earlier in the evening. Bob was hungry and growing desperate. They wandered down to the bakers to see what they could find. The cockroaches had to be cleared before bob could get near the food. Bob was hungry and filled his can until he couldn't get any more in. Back at the house he stripped without being told and started eating his food. Within ten minutes he ate the whole can full. Alf wasn't so sure and didn't want another repeat of the illness. He reached for the bottle of Cod Liver Oil and half filled the can. "I'm OK said bob but Alf wasn't having any arguments. "Kneel, he said. Head back mouth open wide." He poured the oil straight into Bob's mouth and as Bob struggled to drink it he poured out another large dose and poured that into Bob's mouth. "There that should help." He picked up the case and stepped outside as Bob started to break up the pieces of his darkroom for the fire.

The next day Alf retrieved the case with the suit and all the other clothing took it to the pawnbroker who said he'd just sold two suits very much like this one. He called in on Bob to see if he was alright but Bob was fine. "In that case I think its time that you took a bath, you're beginning to smell. Come up to the flat after going around the town. He left Bob the dress and went back to his work.

Bob arrived at the flat after dark shivering from the cold night air. Alf told him to run a bath and while he was in the bath Alf said that a meal would be waiting for him. Half an hour later he was wrapped in two large fluffy Bath towels and tucking in to a plate of ham and eggs. After he'd finished Alf told him to rest and sent him to bed. Bob dropped the towels and Alf noticed how thin he looked but said nothing. Bob was asleep in minutes and Alf gave him a shake but bob wasn't to be awakened. Alf smiled and went to the desk taking out the bottle of ink and a small brush and a ruler. He pulled the bed sheets from bob and turned him onto his front leaving all of his back exposed, and then stated to measure out his back with the ruler and pen by marking little dots on Bob's skin. When satisfied he set to work with the indelible ink and with the brush started to lettering all down his back.

The letters showed up against his white skin tone and Alf went over them again until all the letters were a jet black in colour and would take ages for them to wear off. Satisfied Alf put the ink away and let Bob sleep. With just a day to go the timing must be right. Alf wasn't in the flat when Bob awoke on the Wednesday morning. It was nice to be in his flat with the bathroom and the heating and plenty of food. He found a note from Alf that there was steak and chips in the kitchen waiting for him and to clean up the flat and Alf would be back this evening. Alf meantime was scouring the second had market for a black handbag and a coat. The handbag was soon found but the coat was the problem and he had to settle for a half length one. It was placed into a carrier bag and he went back to work to finish his shift.

Wednesday evening the meal was a stew that they shared. Alf asked how Bob was feeling and had he fully recovered from his illness. He feared that Alf was going to send him back to the house to suffer again and the weather was turning colder but he was wrong and Alf said that we must build your strength up as you had worried me when you collapsed. I'll continue letting you stay here but you better take your stomach powder just in case. Alf went the cupboard and took out a paper and opened it to reveal a white powder.

"Open wide," he told Bob, and then poured the powder in and Bob swallowed it. With the meal over Alf suggested that they have an early night said that he'd give bob a stand up wash. Bob got the hot water as Alf undressed him and started to lather him with shampoo. As each part was washed Alf gave him little kisses and moved down his body kissing each part until he finally took his manhood into his mouth and began licking and sucking and then picked bob up and took him to the bed where he dried his feet and laid him down and climbing in beside him. Bob gave a little yawn and reached for Alf as he responded to the kissing. Alf then turned him over and pulled up to a kneeling position but couldn't bring himself to finish the job. Bob realised what was happening and wanted Alf to do it as it would even the score between them but Alf struggled with either doing the act or his conscience. "Just do the f**king job", he shouted until Alf finally managed. And both collapsed and rested. Bob was already falling asleep. Alf gave him a half an hour and shook him and shouted at him until he was convinced Bob was fully asleep. He threw back the covers and examined the writing on Bobs back noting that the lettering was still jet black in spite of the washing. Now he started again with his bottle of ink and the first thing that was painted on to Bob's front was a bra and then he drew a thin line over each shoulder and another at the sides. Alf examined the painting and noted with satisfaction that it did look as though bob was wearing a bra. Next to be painted on was a girdle with straps going down his legs and then a pair of knickers. When he had finished Alf stood back and couldn't help but smile at his handiwork. The second phase of his plan was finished.

A shrill ringing noise brought Alf to his senses. The alarm was trying to throw itself off the dresser. Alf reached out and bashed it on its head and it quietened down. He'd about two hours to finish the job and hadn't any time to lose. After a quick breakfast of cereals he went to the big chest and took out the black dress along with all the underwear and started to dress bob who was still fast asleep. He managed to put on the bra and girdle but struggled with the nylons and slip. The black dress was fastened and the shoes placed on his feet but then came the difficult part and that was the make up. Alf managed the nails and the lipstick but the eye shadow didn't look right. He tried again and decided it would have to do as time was pressing. He dressed and went out going to town until he reached the taxi cab rank and approach one of the cabmen.

"My mate has to get to the station to catch a train to Glasgow for his National service. The trouble is we were at a party for him and as a joke they have put him into a dress and it's only an hour to the train can you help. He's still out cold, I think that they have put something in his drink and now I can't move him." The cabby had a word with his mate and said that two of them could and would Alf pay for the extra man and Alf agreed.

Bob was lifted into the cab and down to the station. One man got a trolley and bob was loaded onto it and wheeled into the ticket office. Alf took out the voucher and obtain the ticket. Alf thanked them and they left after being paid for their trouble. Alf now sort out a porter and asked for his help to get Bob onto the train. After Alf told him that there would be five shillings for his help the man agreed. The train arrived and the porter had a quick word with the guard and soon Bob was in his seat still fast asleep. The guard tied a ticket onto bob say he was going to Glasgow and his coat and bag were left. The guard said that he would make sure that bob would be handed over to the Army. Alf tipped them and then returned to the flat with a big grin on his face. He would have loved to see the faces of men who were collecting the new recruits at

Glasgow. It would be even better when Bob had to strip for his kitting out or medical because the ink would take weeks to wear off and on Bob's back Alf had written slogans such as: 1720 an Englishman invented the kilt. The Scots still haven't got the joke. Scotsmen are hard, or a better word is thick. The Scotsmen are going to love him for that and the letters will stay on for weeks. Alf had taken his revenge. When Bob finally awoke he found a letter from Alf that read; Thanks' Bob now were even. I've given you your jewellery back along with a fiver that your mum gave to me when she emptied the safe. I didn't want you to lose it so I put it in a condom and stuffed it up your bum. Enjoy yourself in Scotland. By the way it was me who cancelled your deferment and asked for you to be sent to a highland regiment.

All the best Alf.

Alf signed on in the Army to do thirty years service and made Sergeant.

Bob served his two years and then emigrated.

CHAPTER 7

SLAVE

At the ripe old age of eleven going on twelve I decided that things had to change for me. Times were very hard in the country and prospects for an unskilled worker were not good. I would be leaving school in three years to a life of manual labour and low paid working and didn't want either. Being a rent boy was ok and it got the family some money to improve life but the older I got the fewer clients I would get as there were always younger boys coming through. At the age of eighteen I will be conscripted into the armed forces as all boys were but to me that would be just a waste of time. I wanted something more than this life of slavery, and then it struck me. If I was stuck with a life of slavery why don't I become one?

People may tell me that slavery has been abolished and is now illegal but what about voluntary slavery? If I could sell myself into slavery by some scheme and any money be saved in trust for me when I eventually got my freedom, then would that be illegal? I decided to talk it over with my mum who realised that I would shortly have to give up being a rent boy.

Mum was dead against it saying that it was a daft idea but as I gave her the outline of a scheme she started to realise that it could work but had to be checked with a solicitor. We made an appointment for a quick visit where we could talk over any problems we had in a half hour visit and get some advice. Ten days later we presented ourselves at the office of one of the town's leading solicitors we had chosen from the yellow pages. The solicitor we were shown in to see was very young and probably newly qualified as the juniors of the firm would be used for half hour visitors as they couldn't afford to pay a lot. The man asked us to call him Robert and appeared to be very friendly. I wondered if he would stay friendly when he knew what we wanted. "What's your problem?" He asked.

"Is it possible to have legal slavery," mum asked. "Can anyone volunteer to sell oneself into a form of slavery without it becoming illegal?" Robert looked up in amazement. "I don't know but if you could, but think of all the dangers that it could bring, you could be used for sexual purposes for instance." Both I and mum had to smile at that analogy. "We would have to devise a scheme that protects both you and the person who would eventually buy you and what would happen if you got injured and couldn't work, and what about your National Service? I think that this plan of yours will take a lot of working out; I'll have to consult my partners. Can we make another appointment and give me some time to look into things?" With that the interview was over. We had given him a lot of things to see about and the first thing was can a scheme like this be legal. Two week later saw them back in Robert's office.

"As far as we can tell there's nothing to prevent you from your plan but it would have to be like an ordinary contract for a domestic servant with the only difference being the terms and conditions. We wouldn't recommend you try to sell yourself to any country but just to those that we think are safe such as The United States of America. Their minimum working age is sixteen therefore you would have to go to school."

"What about part time schooling at home?" Mum asked.

"You could enrol for a four year part time college course but who would pay?" Robert asked. We had the money from my work as a rent boy but that was needed elsewhere.

"We would have to deduct the college fees from the purchase price that we got from the client. We see the contract being for a five year period and then the client would either cancel the contract or pay for another five years. If we gave them the option at the start then they'd know exactly how much it would cost for every five year period.

Robert thought about it for a moment and then said; "That would work but now we will have to find out what the client would require of you. I'll pass your request along to our London branch to get their opinion and I'll let you know in two weeks." We left the office a little more hopeful as I didn't think the plan would be allowed in any form but now there was some hope.

Two weeks later we were back in Robert's office.

"I've had some feedback from our London branch. It seems that they're intrigued by your proposal and have contacted some of their American friends and this is what they say: To make the scheme work you would have to commit yourself to becoming as near a real slave as it is possible within today's laws. This would mean working for 24/7 although your contract would only allow you to work as a domestic servant you would be on call for the rest of the time that you weren't at school. You will probably be dressed as a slave and may be required to wear any costume that your client wishes you to wear however much or as little as they want. The only exception would be for a school uniform. You may be required to wear a collar. They will have the right about all aspects of your appearance. They will probably want some kind of discipline procedure put into place and a full medical history along with an examination and blood tests. and apart from those conditions you can go ahead as long as you know what you are getting yourself into, what do you think?"

"We will agree to the tests but what would the discipline be?" Mum asked.

"It would have to be of a financial penalty agreed between the client and your solicitors." Robert replied. "That sounds very serious but what about minor things. The client wouldn't want to go running to a solicitor for every little thing so what if we agreed a client using physical punishment for small misdemeanours."

"That would work but it would have to be between you and the client as it is against the law." Robert sat back in his chair. "I think that just about cover's everything. If you wish to go ahead we can leave the fee arrangements to London who will do some advertising through word of mouth among some trusted people that they know." With that the meeting was over and I was committed to becoming a slave.

A letter arrived with an appointment for a full medical with blood tests and then a photo session to follow. It was to be at a private hospital fortunately not too far from where we lived. On the day I had to report to a private room where I stripped and waited while lying on a table. All kinds of test were done and I was prodded and poked in every place of my body and needles pushed into me and samples going back out. At last they had finished and it was off to the photographer who made me strip naked while he took photographs from every angle and then we were done.

A month went by when mum and I were sent tickets to travel to London. We were met by a young man from the London solicitors who had arranged a meeting with possible clients. The meeting was at a posh hotel in the heart of the capital and we travelled by taxi. After being given a meal we waited in a big lobby and then were led to a large room where six gentlemen were seated. A man introduced me and then I was questioned about what I expected and warned what to expect if I didn't do as ordered and how I would feel about wearing a costume all the time. The man who introduced me then said that it had been agreed that any misdemeanour can be punished by a beating on the bottom and a formula agreed for anything of a more serious nature. A beating on the bottom had been agreed, by whom? It was the first time that I'd heard of it.

After going around the gentlemen individually we were told they would be in touch and then the man who had brought us took us back to the station and put us on the train home.

We heard nothing until a week before Christmas when a car drew up outside. It was Robert who came to say that I had been sold and although I thought that I would start on my twelfth birthday could I possibly start at Christmas as I was to be given to a gentleman's wife as a Christmas present. If I would do that I could spend the next two months until my birthday with no duties and get to know the place. I thought that was fair and agreed after talking it over with mum who simply moved Christmas forwards by a week although I wouldn't be getting any presents as I couldn't take them with me.

Very luckily my new passport had just arrived so I was free to go at any time. With two days to go Robert called round with a parcel and I was to wear this. I opened the parcel and took out a short brown tunic with brown briefs and a pair of sandals. I was not to bring anything with me except for one photograph as everything else will be provided for. He said that I would be picked up tomorrow and taken to Manchester airport where a private plane was waiting to take me to America. I'd never been on a plane and now I was going on a private one. I choose a snap of all the family in a metal frame and could hardly wait until the morning. The next morning I washed and brushed my teeth wondering if the order meant not to bring my toothbrush but I decided against it as I hadn't any kind of bag. I put on the tunic and briefs. It felt odd not having any pants on and no socks; it was also a bit cold so mum gave me a white vest to wear underneath saying that they wouldn't want you to catch a cold while flying over there. About ten the car came for me. I said goodbye and climbed in. At the airport we went to a different entrance from the usual passengers. A brief glance at my new passport and we were through running down to the private area where the plane was waiting. As soon as I was abroad we taxied out to the runway and after a pause we took off. There was just a stewardess and myself on board along with the pilots. I was asked if I wanted anything to eat but said no as I'd just had breakfast. The plane had piston engines as the jet aircraft came later and so the flight would be a long one and the stewardess suggested that I should recline the seat and get some sleep, I said no thank you but reclined the seat anyway and woke up seven hours later. I'd been so excited the night before that I didn't realise just how sleepy I really was. We landed and the air stewardess said that this was just a refuelling stop and then I heard the fuel tankers arrive and begin to refill the tanks. I was given a meal and as it was still dark I couldn't watch what was going on. I finish the meal just in time as we took off again. I found it a bit boring flying in the dark as there wasn't anything to see and so I went back to sleep.

I awoke just as it was becoming light. I must have slept all through the night which wasn't usual for me and I wondered if I had been given a drug to make me sleep for so long. The aircraft was on the ground at a small private airport and the stewardess had the door open and appeared to be waiting for someone. Five minutes later a car drew up close to the plane and I was ushered out as she called out Merry Christmas, and I realised that it was early on Christmas Day. We drove about ten mile's and then turned into the drive of a huge mansion and pulled around to the rear and the garage area. A man came out to meet us and I recognised him as one of the men in the hotel. He asked how I was and enquired about the journey and then said that he wanted to surprise his wife at lunch time and would I stay hidden in the garage until then. I took the "would I stay" to mean stay in the garage. The driver took me into a huge garage with room for at least six cars. He placed two blankets in the front of a radiator and told me to lie down. Later my new owner whose name was Hughes came to see me and said his wife would come to the garage about one. He was very polite and asked if I would mind if he took my clothing as I looked so cute when I was naked that first time that he saw me. I said that I wouldn't mind as it was warm in front of the central heating. I stripped of my tunic and briefs and the vest that mum had made me wear. As I removed it I simply said mum and handed it to him. He gave a little smile and nodded that he understood. He said that I now looked like a slave that had just been brought in. I replied that I should been chained if I've just arrived and a chair may be required for her to sit on as she is bound to start to question me. "A chain and a chair," he muttered and went out. Shortly a man who turned out to be the butler arrived with a kitchen chair and a chain. It had a large ring on the end and he looped it through the radiator and threaded the other end through and brought it over to me and fastened it around my neck and attached the lock. With a cheery "don't go away," he left.

The Hughes family party was in full flow with the children opening their presents when Mr Hughes said that he's got a special present for his wife and presented her with a key and a parcel then said her present is waiting in the garage. She of course was thinking it was a car but as she already had a car she wasn't too thrilled. She thanked him and asked what it was but he said that she had to see for herself. She gave him a little puzzled look but took the key and the parcel and walked over to the garage. As she opened the side door to the garage she was amazed to find a little naked boy sitting on a blanket. Mrs Hughes name was Martha named after her mother. Martha walked over to where I was sat and asked who I was and what was I doing here. I informed her that I was her Christmas present and that I was to be her own little slave that her husband had bought. She sat down on the chair that had been provided for the purpose and started to question me about where I had come from and how had I become a slave. I told about the auction in England and the flight to get here for Christmas and how she could have any costume designed for me to wear. Then she remembered that I was still naked and that the parcel was my clothes. I was handed the parcel and she unlocked the chain so that I could dress. Martha took my hand and led me across to where the party was taking place. Everyone stopped what they were doing at my entrance having been told by Mr Hughes that he had bought a slave boy for his wife. After that there were a hundred questions from the two children a boy two years older than I was and a girl about my age. They were called Greg and Lucy and were equally amazed that you could buy a slave in America. After two hours their butler came and took me away to the servant's wing where I was given a room with a bathroom. It appeared that the butler had been in on the secret as waiting there was a toothbrush and comb and shampoo with soap and towels. The bed had been made up ready for me to use if fact everything that I would need had been provided. The butler told me to address him as Mr George and I was to take a shower and then wait here until I was sent for, with that he left. Around four I was taken to another room where the children Greg and Lucy were playing with their toys. These were not children's toys but adult toys. Greg was seated astride a scrambler motor cycle and Lucy at twelve had a full professional make up case. I think that I'd been taken to see their Christmas gifts and was supposed to be envious. I made the right noises say the gifts were great but Greg didn't seem impressed and had a permanent scowl on his face as though he resented me being there. Lucy on the other hand wanted to try out her skill with the makeup and wanted a volunteer and there was only one other person in the room, me. She had a great time laughing every time she applied more makeup in various shades until Mr George came for me and took me down to the basement where the rest of the staff were sitting down for a meal. The same questions were fired at me as before until we settled down to eat.

I settled in to a steady routine that kept the house and grounds running smoothly under the firm hand of Mr George. After the holiday Mr Hughes would drive to his office of stockbrokers and Mrs Hughes would supervise the house and meals and discuss with the head grounds man what needed doing and in the afternoon visit with her friends and go shopping. This time however she had something more important to do and that was to see about my school uniform and my slave outfit. The school uniform was easy. We arrived at the store, took my measurements and within the hour everything had been bought and packed in the car. Next was an appointment with her dressmaker where more discussions were taking place on an unusual order, my tunic. What length should it be? What material? What colour? Various materials were held against me as the ladies decided what they liked. After two hours we next called on her jewellers where she explained what was required and the jeweller sketched out various designs but they settled on a plain band of gold. I was going to be given a slave collar.

Two more weeks passed and both Greg and Lucy had gone back to school and my college course was due to start on the Monday morning. I had already tried on my school uniform and was a good fit but I had to pick up some books that were required. Today the tunics were ready and we set off in the morning around ten. When we were show into a fitting room there were five tunics waiting for me. Two were just plain brown to use in the house but the other three were made from a rich looking material. There was one red, one blue, and one of white, all with trim in a contrasting colour. They looked like costumes for royalty. All had matching briefs and were very short in length. I was told to try each one and was sent into the changing room. The only way they could be put on was by putting them over my head as no zips or buttons had been provided. I stepped out wearing the blue tunic to smiles and polite applause from the staff. They wouldn't have booed would they? The white one made me look like a Roman emperor but Mrs Hughes said that it needed white sandals or the effect would be spoiled. The five tunics were packed and placed into the car and then it was off to the jewellers. I was told to take off my brown tunic and sit on a stool in the work-shop. There a gold collar in two halves was placed around my neck. At each end were two holes and the jeweller insert a round piece of rod shaped like a bullet. He did the same at the other side and then fitted the two halve together. The halves fitted perfectly and Martha gave her approval. The ring was taken off and an assistant brought in a flask that steamed slightly. He said that it was Nitrogen at an extremely low temperature. He lowered four more of the little bullets into the nitrogen and waited a few moments and then wrapped a cloth around my neck. Taking the bullets from the flask with a pair of pliers he picked up one of the now frozen bullets and inserted it into one of the holes in the collar. Soon all four were fitted into the holes and the jeweller wearing heavy gloves picked up the other half of the collar and pressed the two together. A small clamp was put on and I was told not to move as the bullets warmed up. After ten minutes the clamp was taken away and he then tried to pull the collar off but as they had warmed up the bullets being a little oversized had now expanded and sealed the joints of the collar for ever. The only way that collar could be removed was for it to be cut off. The jeweller gave it a little polish and invited Mrs Hughes to examine it. I was given a mirror to have look and I couldn't see the joint. It appeared like a solid ring of gold about a centimetre thick with the top and bottom edges slightly bevelled. I now had a slave collar.

We arrived back at the house at lunchtime. After lunch Mr George told me to change into the brown loincloth and briefs. I was a little self-conscious going about in the loincloth but didn't have a choice. I was paraded in front of Mrs Hughes who seemed to approve and was told that at home I had to wear a loin cloth during the day and a brown tunic for the evening. If they were having company then I would be told which of the coloured tunics to wear.

On the Monday Paul the chauffer drove me to the college to start my course. He told me that he was training to be a teacher but had took to drinking to help him get through the pressure and as a result had dropped out from his teachers training. With Mr Hughes help he now was in recovery and planning to return to his course in another year. He also said that he would assist in my work should I need extra tuition. It was good to know for as I looked through the course books there was one on Algebra and we didn't take that at my old school.

Mr George gave me two sets of cotton underwear as sometimes in California it can get quite cold and now I had the underwear it helped when I was taken out. I'd become accustomed to the loincloth and never thought about it as I went about. The house staff also got used to me and became friendly. The house work was very easy but the school work was growing harder and I had to go to Paul to help me keep up with the rest of the class who thought it very funny to have a slave as their school mate.

The months passed and by summer Greg was due to leave his high school at sixteen and go into higher education and then from there on to University. Mr Hughes said the family had been invited to a cruise in the Caribbean by one of his colleagues before Greg left and that we were all invited, and that included me. We took the plane down to the Caribbean and boarded the yacht. I had a little cabin of my own which was as big as a cupboard but that didn't matter as I'd have never got here on my own. Every body wore swimsuits during the daytime and we swum and had picnics on the beach and had waterskiing. We went snorkelling and scuba diving was just coming in but we didn't have on board. I was as brown as a berry when the time came for us to return home and then it was back to college and the hard slog until Christmas. Even Greg had cheered up and was sometimes pleasant to me.

That Christmas I was to be Big Ted. This was a large Teddy Bear that a small person or a boy could climb into and move about much to the delight of the children who had been invited to the annual children's party. Just as the kids were ready to finish their lunch Mr George brought in Big Ted. The head unzipped from the neck and could be taken off. I had to strip to my briefs and climb into Big Ted through the neck and then the head was replaced and zipped up. I was asked to stand and walk around but couldn't rise without help because the arms and legs were padded and wouldn't bend. After being helped I stood and tried to walk which I did but looked more like a toy soldier that a teddy, still lets hope the children didn't notice. I walk into the big room and was mobbed by kids who all seemed to want to sit on me. I was knocked to the floor by a swarm of kids. I couldn't get up and with all the padding it was growing very hot in the suit. Mr George finally rescued me and after that I stayed close to the wall to prevent falling. It wasn't until tea that I could wave goodbye and walk out of the room to be taken from the suit. Mr George said that I'd done a splendid job and he would book me again for next year.

The summer came around as it usually did. Mr Hughes announced that we would be going on a tour around Europe He did mention the we would be making an overnight stop for fuel and to restock the aircraft at Manchester with just a chance that I could make a quick trip home to see my mum as we could only send letters. I wrote to mum that I'd be coming but could only stay for a couple of hours before flying off to Paris. Lucy kept asking me what it was like in Paris but I'd never been out of the country before and could only tell her what I'd read. We landed at noon and a car was arranged for me to go over the Pennines'. The trip lasted two hours and all the family was waiting. I was in my brown tunic that was to me quite normal but to mum made her smile as it was so short. I took a load of photo's to show her as I'd borrowed a camera and snapped everything and everybody. Two hours later I was in Manchester once again and had to share a twin room with Greg who didn't like that as he thought I was beneath him but as the hotel was full he'd no choice.

We did Paris next and all the tourist spots and it was on to Berlin, Warsaw, Madrid, and Athens and across the Med to Egypt to the pyramids and back to London. We flew from London to the states. It had been a wonderful trip and one I'd remember for a long time. Greg turned sixteen and had a big party at the house. His present was a brand new car so that he could drive himself to his new High School, his last before University.

Lucy was in trouble with her father. She had been picked up in a bar drinking with men and she wasn't yet fourteen but with her makeup looked a lot older. I turned fourteen in the New Year. I was halfway through college with the help of Paul and now was beginning to enjoy most of the work. One night I was just finishing my homework when one of the maids knocked on my door to say that Lucy wanted me. I put away my work and went over to the other wing of the house and up to Lucy's room where I knocked on the door. Lucy was lying on the bed and said that she had something in her eye and could I get it out. I leaned over and placed my hand on her pillow for support as I tried to raise her eyebrow to have a look in her eye. She pushed me up a little and I thought that she was making herself more comfortable when she suddenly gave a violent shove that turned me over onto my back and with her left hand grabbed my groin in a vice like grip and squeezed with her long fingernails digging in until I gasp and called out please don't.

Lucy gave a wicked smile and said "look up to your right. Do you see anything? "Handcuffs." "Put your wrist into them and close them." She gave a little squeeze until I did like she asked. Then with her right hand she reached across to the other side where another set was hanging from the bed. "Other hand please." I obliged and soon the hand was secured and at last the grip loosened. "What are you doing?" I enquired. "Shagging you." Then she reached for the loincloth and loosened it and dragged it down to my ankles along with the cotton underwear. Lucy stood and walked to the bottom of the bed where my sandals were taken off and then each leg was fastened to the corners of the bed. I was totally exposed and at her mercy. Lucy then stripped off and climbed onto me.

"Now don't be shy, lets see how proud you are." She grabbed my penis and began to stroke and squeezed me until I had to give way and stood proud. "Well, we can't let that go to waste can we?" She lowered on to me and began to rock gently going faster and faster. I didn't have any choice but to lie there and take it. After a while she was satisfied but still kept me tied to the bed. I was fearful that I would be missed and pleaded to be set free. After an hour I was released and allowed to dress. I got back to my little room and took a shower and examined myself. There were marks showing where her fingernails had dug in and they had drawn blood.

It started to become a regular thing that Lucy would send for me and then use me for sexual purposes. Mr George had his room in the same wing as Lucy and I was sure if it went on that he would get to know. Greg too had his room which was the first one along the corridor but he was away at his high school for most of the time.

On Saturday evening Greg had returned home for a break at one of the short holidays that happen in the States. Lucy had just released me from what had become a duty and I was leaving her room. As I was passing Greg's room the door opened and he called out come in here. I entered and was told to close the door. He said that I'd never shown him the respect that he should have as the son of the house but now that was going to change. He knew what was going on between me and his sister and it was in his power to have me dismissed and sent back home without a penny. He brought out a photograph of me and Lucy naked on the bed making love. The picture was taken from a high position, possible the light fitting. I didn't know what to say. We had been found out and it remained to see what Greg wanted to do with the evidence.

"You do realise that anything you do to me you also do to Miss Lucy." Greg smiled and replied. "I don't want to do anything to either of you but from now on I'm your Master and you'll obey my every word or else the picture will go to father and that means the end of you. Lucy will get over it."

I knew he'd got me and for the time being I was trapped. "You may go for now," said Greg. "Yes Master." I replied. Greg smirked as I left his room. The next day I sort out Lucy and told her what Greg had done. After she had calmed down we looked for the place where the camera had been installed but couldn't find it, then I had an idea. The camera didn't have to be a full size camera it could be one of those spy cameras that just needed a tiny hole for the lens. We searched again and found a spot where there was a small hole next to the light fitting.

Lucy had a word with the maintenance man about hearing noises above the ceiling. He went up to the attic and said that there had been someone up there and a floorboard had been lifted but there was nothing to see now. He said that maybe someone had been checking the electrics for safety purposes. Lucy said that was probably it and the man went away satisfied. We knew that it had been a rat, a two legged rat that had been up there. Greg left to go back to his course but I knew that he would be back. I had a word with Paul and told him what had happened but was advised not to do anything but if Greg wanted to be called Master, well, I'll call him master and boost his ego as it can't hurt and he'll be away at University soon. That's true I thought as all course would end in the summer and the new ones would start in the autumn. My course would also end and my schooling would be over as I would be turning sixteen. The maintenance man reported that the hole had been blocked up and the floorboards had been nailed down and Lucy should have no more trouble.

That summer we all holidayed on a ranch and went camping and horse riding in the Rockies. Greg didn't join us and for once I was thankful that he wanted to go with his friend from school. Lucy was back to her old self a loving sweet young girl always ready for a laugh and a joke. Mr and Martha Hughes seem more relaxed and I got saddle sore from too much riding that caused Lucy to break out in more laughter. Too soon the holiday passed and it was time to get back to studying for my last term at school. It rained all the way back and it was just how I felt. I had just four more moths to endure.

Two weeks before Christmas Greg returned. His schooling was over and he was waiting for his University courses to start in the summer and meantime he had time on his hands. I had just the final exams to complete the course and they would start next week but I still had home work to do. One Friday the week before the finals I had just finished my homework on Algebra a subject I always had a problem with. It was after nine and I heard a noise in the corridor. Mr Hughes and his wife was at a charity function so I wondered who was making the racket when my door burst open and in walked Greg and three of his friends from school. Nobody not even Mr George walked into a room without being asked. Everyone knocked politely on the door and waited to be invited in even Mr Hughes. I stood at the surprise visit and then one of the group said; "Is this him then." Greg smirked that annoying smirk of his and nodded. "Yes this is my slave." I was going to reply that I was his father's slave but then remembered the photograph. Greg had obviously come to show off to his mates and as I could smell alcohol on their breaths I thought it better than to argue. "Let's have a better look at him then." Greg walked right in front of me and said strip for the gentlemen. I could have said that I don't see any gentlemen here but that would just cause more trouble. I could have refused but what if he carried out his threat to show the snap out of spite. I decided to go along with him and pulled off my tunic. "And the rest," he said pointing to the briefs. I reluctantly pushed off the briefs and because I was already bare footed I stood before them naked. "This is his slave collar then," someone said stating the obvious. "How does it come off?" Greg had an audience and that pleased him. "It doesn't come off. It wouldn't be a slave collar if it came off." He told them. The other man wouldn't leave the subject. "Well how did he get it on?"

Greg didn't know and turned to me. I said "Nitrogen." "There" said Greg "It was Nitrogen." Without either of the pair having a clue what was Nitrogen.

"Can you shag him if you want?" The big one of the group asked. "I can if I want but I just don't want." "Well I fancy him do you mind if I shag him." Greg smirked once again. "Go ahead if you want to. Greg turned to me. Get on the bed." He ordered. The big fellow those name was Jack was already taking down his pants. The last thing I wanted to do was to give satisfaction to Greg but I was in a bit of a spot and had to make my mind up whether to obey or not. I decided at this time I had no option so I reluctantly lay down on my bed. Jack was a big man in that he was fully grown being around six feet tall and weighing about 200lb and not of fat but young muscle. Not only that his penis was also huge and by far the largest that I've ever had to take even when I was a rent boy. His weight pushed me to the bed so I could hardly move and I felt him probe me as he searched for the opening, then suddenly he found it and pushed into me giving me a tremendous pain the caused an involuntary cry from my lips. I could imagine Greg smiling again but I'd more to think about just then. Jack was enjoying himself but I suffered until with a final grunt he finished. "Nice shag," he said as he got up and went to the bathroom and used my face towel to clean himself. Greg was pleased. He had demonstrated his power and now he was going to show more power. I was next ordered to kneel before him and give him oral sex. Well I though I've come this far so I may as well. Greg had that smirk on his face as he made me kneel in front of him. I so wanted to give him a good smack in the face although he was a lot bigger than me it would be well worth it, but there was Lucy to think about and so I was forced to submit. He held my head during the oral sex and then as he reached his climax he stopped me from withdrawing and I had a mouthful of the vile liquid, and then he slapped me hard on my back and caused me to involuntary swallow. He saw that caused me some distress and laughed at my dilemma. After Greg the other two plucked up the courage to ask for oral sex and of course I had to oblige.

All four had used me for sex and I thought that finally they would go and leave me in peace, but no, Greg wasn't finished with me yet. He picked up my homework and asked what this was. I told it was my homework that I had to do for my college course. He took the top page and told me to fold it in half. Then I had to fold it in half again and then again until it wouldn't fold any more. He ordered me to open it out and tear it up on the fold creases until it was in little pieces. He then ordered me to flush it down the lavatory. This really got to me as it had taken half the night to complete the work. I think that he sensed that he had at last hurt me because he then ordered me to tear all the work into small pieces and throw then down the lavatory where he flushed them away.

I heard them laughing and joking as they went down the corridor after first trashing the room. Paul entered and looked at the mess and asked what they did to me. I told that I'd been raped and used for sex had the room trashed and all the homework flushed down the toilet. I was as close to tears as I could be. The act with my homework really upset me. Paul told me to take a shower while he helped with the room. When I'd dried and put on a pair of briefs I came out of the shower to find half the staff working away at changing the bed, picking everything up and packing it away and Paul half way through my homework saying just copy this out I know that you did it right the first time. The tears began to flow. How can you get people like Greg who are proper shits and then other's like the staff at the house and Paul who will go out of their way to help.

One month later the four were back. It was just after Christmas that the four returned and they must have though that they needed a laugh as a New Years present. My door banged open and in they walked with Greg leading them. Before they had the chance to order me to strip a voice stopped them in their tracks.

"What are you doing here?" It was Mr George. Greg went pale. Mr George turned to him. "You know the rules as well as any, the staff quarters are out of bounds to everyone. Not even your father comes down here. Now what do you want?" Greg didn't know what to do or say. If you can't remember you better go and take your friends with you and don't come here again." The four turn and fled from the corridor. Paul came out with a huge smile on his face. Mr George turned to me. "Don't let them interfere with you ever again. If they ask refer them to me." "I couldn't sir." I was going to tell him about the blackmail when he said to the rest of the staff; Leave us and then he closed the door so that nobody could hear. "If you're worried about the photograph then don't be. We know all about it and about Miss Lucy. You see Miss Lucy is a wonderful girl but she does have a problem. I'm telling you this in the strictest confidence and it mustn't go any further. She was found soliciting for men in a down town bar when she was thirteen years old. Fortunately the police found her and brought her home. She is what's known as a, he paused and said let's put it this way. She like men, lots of men and will do anything to have them. It's an illness just like any other and you just happened to be available. However you did suit our purpose you see she likes you and I think you like her and while she's with you she's not running away going to bars and with god knows who. It was wrong of us to use you in that way but we are desperate. If you don't want to help then we'll stop it immediately but it means Miss Lucy will have to be locked up for her own good."

"That explains a lot" I said. I'll be glad to help as long as I don't get caned or dismissed. After I get me results I'll have finished my schooling and I'll have more time to be with her as long as Master Greg leaves me alone." "Leave Master Greg to me. He has to explain putting up the cameras in Lucy's room and then there are a few other things his father wants to know about such as drugs, you haven't taken any have you." "No sir, I haven't." "Good boy, now I must go and make sure that those idiots have left the house." Mr George turned and strode down the corridor. Paul must have been listening as he opened his door and gave the thumbs up sign to me. For a present Mr Hughes said that Paul could start teaching me to drive around the estate's roads and when I was competent I would get a driving instructor and use of a car when I passed.

With Greg away at University and Lucy under a little bit of control at home life settled down to the same routine. I was spending more time with Lucy as instructed but enjoyed her company. Martha decided not to send her to higher education but found her a part time job working for a charity in the morning and the work appeared to do her good as she became her old loveable self. On the odd occasion I would be handcuffed to the bed as she had her way with me but in a nice way.

Greg returned after university and started work in his fathers firm but quit after a year and took a flat to be away from his father's control. After two years he got married but it didn't last and ended in a messy divorce and then he wed for the second time only to have that marriage break down. He turned to drugs once again and spends his time without a job snorting cocaine to pass the days. It's said that he is running out of funds through his drug habit and is selling his goods to make ends meet.

Lucy eventually also married and her marriage broke down and ended in divorce. She too left home and has a house a few miles from the old home. Lucy Has plenty of money as she receive a handsome payout as a settlement from her divorce.

Martha died of cancer a few years ago and left Mr Hughes at a loss as he misses her so. I stayed with him until he was over seventy when he suddenly died, some say of a broken heart. Neither Greg nor Lucy wanted to return to the estate and the house was closed down. The workers were laid off and my option which had a year to run was cancelled and I was freed but it meant that I had no where to go to. I'd been a slave for twenty four years and hadn't a home other than the house and my mother and some friends from home were also gone. I returned home but the house had been pulled down and the rest of the family dispersed and so I returned to the USA and bought a house a little way from the old place. The house was near to where Paul was now teaching and Mr George had bought a small hotel and bar where he engaged some of the old staff. I myself married one of the staff from the old days and we both now work for Mr George. On a Friday night we all get together and talk of the old days. I've got plenty of memories and also still wear my slave collar.

CHAPTER 8

FROM HIM TO HER

Alone at last, in my own room, with my own furniture even if it was donated and not worth much, at least it's mine. I can do as I want, go where I please, decide what to eat and when to eat, so different from the children's home with it's rules and regulations even if we didn't always obey them. Now at sixteen the time had come to leave.

It was five years ago since my parents were killed in a car accident and having no relatives or money I was put into care, a shy sensitive lad crying himself to sleep. Stop that, they said, you're too big to cry. Well I didn't feel too big.

For five years there's been an uneasy truce between the home and myself but now freedom, but at the same time an odd feeling of loneliness. There was always someone at the home to talk to, so much so that at times you longed for piece and quiet, but now there's no one here but me. Food, it's time to eat, but what? The after care will help for another two years if need be but I need them now. Who's going to make me a meal? The little gas cooker is equipped with two pans for me to cook with but nobody taught me to cook. Well, it'll have to be beans for tonight.

The little drawer in the cupboard holds the cutlery. Oh no, there's no opener. Never mind I'll make do with toast for now. Wonder what there doing back at the home. Watching the tele I'll bet. Well I'm not bothered I've got better things to do.

Right, let's have a look at these forms they've given me to fill in. First question. Name and address. Raymond, my name is Raymond, and my address is printed on the top of this bloody silly form. Why ask if you knew already oh, to Hell with it. I'll do it tomorrow when I sign on at the Job Centre. Best thing to do is to go to bed it's been a long day.

Da Da Da, Di Da Da. I know that song, it's from that new group starting out. Ray listened to the music coming through the wall from the next room. It must be on the television. Never mind I'll save up and get one soon. It's getting cold in here, no central heating; I might as well go to bed.

Raymond stripped off his shirt and washed at the small hand basin. He took off his shoes and socks and folded his jeans and caught sight of himself in the long mirror on the old fashioned wardrobe door. A slim bordering on thin little boy stared back. He was sixteen last Saturday but looked about twelve. Ever since the crash he'd simply stopped growing. All his pals in the home and his school mates towered above him. They gave him the name RUNT, then RAT and finally RATTY. Well it didn't matter now. He climbed into bed in his underwear, the bed clothes felt cold and remembered for the thousandth time how his mother had tucked him in and gave him a goodnight kiss, well no kiss for him tonight as he turned over and tried to sleep.

Breakfast was cornflakes and milk washed down with a mug of tea. He slept surprisingly well considering it was a strange new place. The first thing to do is to buy a can opener then there's that silly form to take in. If the money holds out I'll have a curry tonight but first sign on.

It took an age to finish all the various forms and complete his signing. Why not send the letters the home had given him straight to the Job Centre and save him the trouble. The same forms have now to be filled in for Social Security. Ray was muttering to himself as he scanned the Vacancy Boards .

Wanted, School leaver, the notice caught his eye. 'What's this?' He thought as he read the card. Shop fitter, he'd no idea what a fitter did but It was a local firm and the pay sounded good when in fact it was low. He made a note of the number and took it to the desk.

The young lady on the desk took the card number and punched the details up on her computer. "It's a Shop fitter" she said, "and local to you," as though that was the first time he'd seen the card. "Would you like me to give them a ring for you." She asked. Ray nodded. The young lady rang a number and talked to someone on the phone. "Is three this afternoon all right?" He was unsure of whom she meant. She looked at him and raised her eyebrows. He nodded once more. "Yes, right then, yes right, that'll be fine, he'll see you at three, bye." and put the phone down. "I've made you an appointment this afternoon at three," she said to Ray as though he hadn't heard the phone call. "This is the address," pointing to the card. I know, I know, he felt like shouting but instead nodded once more. He picked up the card and left.

Ray stopped at the local store for his can opener, added some eggs and ham and frozen chips for the small freezer compartment in his fridge. Now he could have a good fry - up before getting ready for his appointment.

His one good suit in the wardrobe was laid out onto the bed after lunch. A good wash and don't forget to clean the teeth. His teeth were good, nice and white and even. That was one good thing about the home they made you clean your teeth and sent you for regular checks. At two, he dressed, brushed his hair and being only a short distance decided to walk to his appointment. One hour later he had a position as a shop fitter, well a learner shop fitter. Definitely a curry night he thought.

Monday morning he put on his jeans and trainers and walked to his new job. A few men were already in the works yard when he arrived. Well, look what we've got here, its little Ratty. Ray turned towards the direction of the voice and recognised an older boy who had been at the same school. Dam, he thought, now I'm stuck with that bloody nickname.

The charge hand came out of the office and gave instructions to the men. Half an hour later the wagon was loaded, the men climbed aboard and his work had begun.

Manchester, City Centre, he read the signs as they passed.

They followed until stopping at a run down shop. Boards were placed around the wagon and unloading started. Now he found out what shop fitting meant. At day's end the place looked like a bomb site. The old shop had been torn apart with all the old woodwork taken out. Cables hung loose, doors were off and floorboards removed. All Ray had done was to bring and carry, still as long as he was paid who cares.

At the end of the week stood a brand new shop with shiny new counters and doors with new fitting's all round, re-wired and freshly painted, so ended week one. It was pay - day for the men but he would have to work a week in hand

and would have to get manage on his Social money. Week two saw him back in the centre again doing a solarium above a ladies hair salon.

The owner, Mrs Mather and daughter Margaret worked in the shop below whilst the solarium was being built upstairs. "Hello Ratty," said Margaret smiling, she must have heard the name from one of the men. "I'm Margaret, you can call me peg. Would you like some cake?" Peg was about his age but a good six inches taller. Her hair was cut in a short boyish style and like him wore T - shirt and jeans with trainers. He took the cake without a word and bit into it, the cream filled his mouth. "Where are you from? Peg enquired. He told her of the crash and the children's home and just starting work. "Are you sixteen then, you don't look it, we thought you were one of the men's son, just passing time. When's your birthday." "March 6th" he said. "Ah! Mine is the third, I'm three day's older than you, and I'm bigger." "That's true," he thought eyeing her shoulders that looked strong. Just then a voice called out Ratty. "I'm wanted, have to go, thanks for the cake."

The solarium was a big job, best part of two weeks. Every day Peg would waylay him with cake and biscuits. He got on well with her and her mother and was invited to tea on the following Sunday. He accepted, it was better than his little room. "Good, Mum will pick you up at four, where do you live?"

Sunday, he was taken to a detached house on the out skirts of the city. Peg introduced him to her Mum's friend Dr Bennet. "Don't complain of anything or he'll have your pants down and cough before you know it." Ray laughed a little self consciously.

The meal over Peg took him up to her room to listen to her records. It was the first time they had been alone. The evening passed quickly until he was called to be taken home, but not before arranging a date to go to a Disco. They drove home to Ray's and Peg got out of the car to see him to the door. She reached and took his face in her hands and gave him a kiss. Her lips were soft and he was a little surprised Peg had made the first move, and then she was gone.

A few weeks later they were up in Peg's room lying on the bed with their feet on the pillows and head hanging over the end of the bed. Peg rose and stood at the end of the bed. Ray rolled onto his back looking up at her. She took hold of his hands and gently pushed them down to his waist, let go , and took hold of his T - shirt and pulled it up over his chest, and leaning over kissed his belly coming slowly up to the chest kissing and giving tiny love bites. He tried to respond and kiss her back but to no avail, Peg wasn't interested. He writhed in pleasure as she stroked and kissed him. Then a call came, time to go. Peg allowed him to give her a kiss as he got into the car.

The week after Ray moved to another house nearer to Peg but still near his work. Now they could be together most nights and at weekends. Their seventeenth birthdays were near. Ray asked, "What would you like for a present?" Peg answered, "A ring." Ray was taken a little aback but the more he thought about it the more he realised he did love her in a sort of way. "An engagement ring? He asked." Peg nodded. He took her in his arms and asked her to marry him, this time taking the lead for once.

The next morning they together chose matching gold rings. "These are like wedding rings wouldn't you like one with stones instead?" Peg smiled, "This is what I want, I don't need a ring with stones." It was Saturday and Peg was due to work in the shop. "Come and have a tan," she said leading him by the arm.

Peg's mum was busy in the salon when they arrived. They were congratulated and kissed after showing the rings.

"I'm going to give Ray a tan." "Yes, all right dear, I can manage down here." Ray was led up to the new solarium, the one he'd helped to build. Outside one of the cubicles he was handed a pair of goggles and a towel. Change in here, I've got some cream to do your back. Ray stripped to his briefs and lay on the sun bed putting his goggles on. The cubicle door opened, Peg entered and sat on the edge of the sun bed. Ray felt the cool cream being put onto his back, the meals Peg's mum had given him had filled him out a little, now he was just slim. Peg worked the cream as a masseur would working down from the neck and shoulders gently kneading and caressing him, down further to the small of his back rubbing in more cream as required until she reached the briefs. With one movement she pulled them down and off. He tried to catch them as he felt them being pulled down but was too late he was lying naked on the bed. His hand was caught and held in a tight grip as Peg dropped some cream onto his buttocks and rubbed it in. She pushed Ray's hand back up to his shoulders and then used both hands to massage him with slow gentle strokes. His legs were pulled open and one hand traced his cheeks going down and down and right under. Ray almost moaned with sheer pleasure.

"Turn over," said Peg, that's this side done." Ray didn't move, after all he was naked. She hooked an arm under his thigh and flipped him over before he knew what was happening. He tried to cover his nakedness but once again his hands were caught and pulled back over his head leaving him totally exposed. More cream across his neck and chest and down his abdomen descending until she grasped his genitals with both hands until she induced an erection. She played with him for a moment until he thought he might burst and then left him rest as her hands continued down the legs.

A kiss told him it was over. "Now you can do me." The T shirt she wore was pulled over her head and her jeans slipped off. Ray watched as she unhooked the fastening of her bra letting it fall to the floor to be followed by her briefs. It was the first time he'd seen her naked, or come to think of it, any woman naked. The cream was passed to him as she lay down He took the cream and tried to do the same as Peg had done to him until finally she pulled him down by her side and her hand ran down his body to grasp and arouse him once again, until this time he was fulfilled.

The months passed. They decided to marry in the December and have a honeymoon at Christmas somewhere warm. Peg's mum and her friend Dr Bennet were going to come too. Ray thought it a little odd but didn't argue as most of the expense was going to be paid by her, and as they were going to a Caribbean island he couldn't afford it on his own.

In the summer a Gymnasium and Health complex was taken over by Mrs Mather, also a second hair dressing shop with a beauty section with massage and sauna. The business was going from strength to strength and both Peg and Mum were busy training new staff. Ray was given a pass to the Gym. "I expect you to use it at least three times a week I want you showing off your muscles on our honeymoon."

He did as he was ordered all through the summer and autumn, however when he looked in the mirror he saw a little boy looking back at him, true no longer thin and with a little more shape to his chest but still looking like a little boy and only one month to the wedding.

The wedding was to be a registry one as only the four of them were to be there. Ray had no friends of his own having lost touch with his former mates in the home. Even the after care people seemed to think he was all right and left him alone. He gave notice to the landlord of his room as after the wedding he would be living with Peg at her house. He packed his suitcase and few belongings. Most of the furniture will go back to the Social. He put on the new suit bought for the wedding, checked his money and passport and did a last look around to see if there was anything left that he wanted. The car arrived; he picked up his bag and closed the door behind him.

They drove home to deposit his bags. His holiday clothes already having been separated and were packed ready to go. "Look what I've bought you," said Peg, holding up a pair of swimming trunks. Ray looked. They were tiny. "I'll never get into those," said Ray. "Of course you will they'll stretch," replied Peg. "Try them we've got plenty of time." "What now!" I've just got dressed for the wedding." "Go on, just to please me."

Ray reluctantly started to undress. Apparently not quick enough for Peg who knocked his hands away and proceeded to undress him herself. His shirt and vest were pulled over his head in one movement not even waiting to unbutton the cuffs. His belt was next. He was unbuckled and unzipped, pushed onto the bed, his shoes socks and trousers came off in one swift movement. She reached for his shorts. "I can manage the rest, turn your back please," said Ray. She smiled at his shyness but turned around. He put on the trunks. "Ready" he said. Margaret turned to regard him. "There," she said triumphantly, "I said they'd stretch." Ray looked in the mirror. Stretch they had. The sides were nearly a single cord, he was showing half his backside and the front was very low cut covering just what it had to leaving a tight little bulge. Peg stooped to examine more closely, reaching up to run her finger over the front of the trunks. "Steady, if I react in these I'll pop out." "You look nice in them, they suit you." "I'd prefer shorts or larger trunks, I feel as though I daren't move or I'll lose them." "Wear them for me, come now it's time to change."

The wedding was over in ten minutes. A meal was prepared back at the house. "I don't feel married." said Ray. "You will." quipped Dr Bennet. He received a dig from an elbow for his trouble, but more in fun than anger. Having eaten they cleared the table and washed the dishes. "Bring your cases down and close the windows." A car drew up. "Taxi's here." Mrs Mather ordered as she fussed around the kitchen. The cases were loaded, the house locked. A steady drizzle started as they headed for the airport but they couldn't care less, they were on the way to sunshine.

The hotel was built on the beach. It had two distinct wings set in a semi - circle facing the sea. Two pools were in front each with sun lounge's, and to the rear golf and tennis. Ray and Peg unpacked. It had been a long flight and both were tired. Dr Bennet and Peg's mum were in the other wing and had also retired for the night. Ray placed his pyjamas on the pillow. "What are those for?" Asked Peg. He cracked the old joke: "In case of fire." Peg smiled, "Come here," and gave him a kiss. "Let me undress you," starting without waiting for an answer. This time he didn't stop her pulling his short's off. Peg undressed herself and lay with him on the bed.

Later he was led to the shower. When it ran warm Peg motioned him to stand in whilst she soaped a flannel and pro-ceeded to give him an all over wash, then stood in the shower and soaped herself. She dried herself and wrapped Ray in a large bath towel patting him dry. "I love having you naked all to myself." He was led back into the bedroom. "Close your eye's," he did so and heard a rustling. "Arm's up," he raised his arm's and felt something drop over them and down his body. "Open," said Peg. He opened his eyes and saw Peg was in his pyjamas and he was wearing her nightie. *"Peg,* he said in protest. She held him close running her hands up and down his back. "You're so pretty I could eat you, let's go to bed." He was led to the bed, the matter of who wore the nightie seem-ingly settled. Ray was by now too tired to argue. Peg held him in her arms and he fell asleep.

In the morning they went down to breakfast in matching short robes and sandals. Peg had on a one piece costume and had made Ray wear the mini trunks. At the pool side he took off his robe. "Cheeky," said Peg's mum. He wanted to cover himself up again and was sure he was blushing. "Doesn't he look pretty," said Peg. Now he was sure he was blushing.

The honeymoon cum holiday passed very quickly. He got used to his trunks but Peg kept to her one - piece suit. On the last night in the hotel a big party was thrown for the guests. Peg dressed in a blue dress Ray suddenly realised this was the first time he'd seen her in a dress as until this evening it was usually jeans or trouser suits.

No pyjamas or nightie was used that night as they lay naked in each others arms.

Christmas in the sun was different and although carols had been sung it just seemed like an ordinary holiday. In the morning on a last walk before the flight home, Peg stopped at a roadside shop selling the usual tourist goods and selected a white dress from the rack. One hour later the bus arrived to take them to the airport for the long flight home. The flight tired them all. Arriving in the early hours they took a taxi home and went straight to bed

On Monday morning Ray reported for work after his three weeks off. He was put to work on a huge store complex. This contract had been going on for some time although he'd been on a different job. Two weeks working on the new store a rumour started spreading. The main contractor had gone bankrupt leaving the small sub - contractors in dire financial trouble. His employer was one of those affected by the bank-ruptcy He was owed thousand's of pounds for material and labour, most of it borrowed from the bank. The firm tried to continue with other work but the interest charges were crip-pling. The workforce was called to the office where a statement was read out to the effect that the firm would have to cease trading and they regrettably were being made redundant. Ray was out of work. The only jobs his mother in law had were all for ladies hairdressing and solarium except for the Gymnasium and they were fully staffed. Ray signed on at the Job Centre once again.

"Hi! Ratty, how's married life?" It was his old workmate also signing. "Better if I had a job." Ray wandered down to the Gym to take his frustration out on the weights, got fed up and returned home.

"Never mind love, something will turn up." Peg put her arm around him as though protecting him. She was right. A month later confirmation came Peg was expecting. Later in their room Peg took the white dress she had purchased on their honeymoon and held it up. "I've never even had it on to see how it looks." "Ray, stand up and hold it in front of you." He was used to being ordered about and knew it was no use protesting. He held the dress up. Peg looked at it walking back and forth studying it from various angles. "I still can't tell, come here. She pulled his shirt over his head. "Try it on for me so I can see." He didn't like to but Peg had dropped his pants and was already putting it over his head. It dropped around his shoulders, his arms were put into the sleeve's and he was zipped up. He stood there looking sheepish in the white mini - dress. Peg sat him on the bed to remove the fallen pants. "It needs something," she said, "I know." Opening the drawer she took out a pair of white knee socks and put them on him. "There, stand up and walk around."

Just then Mrs Mather and the Dr came upstairs. "Mum, come and look." "No! Don't." said Ray. Too late, the door opened and they saw him in the dress.

"Oh, doesn't he look pretty. Turn around and let's look from the back. It suits him but he needs a bosom. Haven't you an old bra he could use"? "No, mine are all too big and he's only a little girl." Replied Peg. "Never mind, I'll get him one for his birthday." Mum said as she and the doctor left.

"Come here," Peg sat Ray on her knee and held his cheek while she kissed him. "Wear it for me, I like to see you in it." Her hand strayed to his knee and started to caress him going higher and higher up his leg under the short skirt. "Let's go to bed."

On his birthday Peg's mother was as good as her word. She gave him a parcel. He opened it up. It contained the promised padded bra also matching briefs with suspender belt and stockings and shoes with high heels.

Peg seemed delighted. He wasn't so sure. "Go try them on to see how they fit," urged Peg. Ray reluctantly made his way upstairs and slowly undressed. The bra wouldn't fasten, he tried the briefs. They were white lace and very flimsy. The door opened. "What's taking you so long?" asked Peg. "It's this bra it won't fasten." "Come here, it's the straps they need adjusting that's all." She moved the straps. "Now try." "Do I have to," wailed Ray, "It doesn't seem right." "Of course it's right, come here." Peg took the bra and put it on him fastening the hook behind. His finger ran over the lightly padded bra as he looked at himself in the mirror. "Here," he was handed the stockings. "Put those on." As he stooped to put the stockings on he felt the suspender belt being placed around his waist.

After the second stocking, Peg adjusted the straps, pushed them through the panties and clipped on the stockings. She helped him with the shoes. "There, at last," she said standing back to see the full effect. "Now hurry with your dress and come down." The door closed behind her.

Ray put the dress on and looked in the mirror at his reflection. A young girl stared back dressed in a white mini - dress. He raised the hem a little eyeing the stocking tops and the ends of the suspender straps. The shoes were higher than he was used to. He took a few tentative steps and nearly twisted his ankle, you just couldn't walk by putting the heel down first, but together, toe and heel he could just manage without overbalancing. He was ready but didn't want to face them. He walked to the door, opened it, he knew he'd no choice but to go down.

"That's better," said Pegs mum as he came down the stairs. She circled him making small adjustments. "A little bit of make-up and with the hair done differently and he would be beautiful. Now remember to keep your legs closed when you sit, you don't want everyone to see what you've got, do you?" Who's everyone, thought Ray, but said nothing. "I've got to go I'm on call, said the doctor. He left as Peg and her mum continued talking about him and totally ignoring the fact he could hear, it was as if he wasn't there. He stood fingering the hem of his dress.

"Can I change now?" Back came the answer. "No, sit down there and don't interrupt." The talking continued as before. Some minutes later a hard slap across his legs stung him out of his reverie. "Keep your legs together, what have you been told." Then he was ignored again as the conversation continued. That night in bed Peg told him she was turned on when he dressed up, and he really was beautiful and to emphasise the point her hand ran up his nightie.

A week later a sign appeared in the garden of the house. It belonged to an estate agent; the house was up for sale. Dr Bennet and Mrs Mather were getting married and all were going to live in one big house. Estate agents brochures began to appear and one or two possibilities were chosen. Weekends would be spent running out in the car looking at properties. Ray was glad it took everyone's minds off dressing him up. He got the job of showing prospective buyers around their home whilst the others were working. Peg was showing her pregnancy now and mother was busy with the business. At last he found a buyer for the house and now the panic set in to find another home for them. Every day would be spent going through the new homes offered for sale without any luck.

One day, at the estate agents office a familiar voice said, "House hunting Ratty?" It was his old workmate standing behind him. Ray told him they were looking for a larger place for the four of them. "Why don't you see old Jenkinson's house, he's going to live abroad."

Jenkinson's house was once a farmhouse but the farm had been sold long ago. It stood surrounded by fields, a large rambling place of six bedrooms with large room's downstairs and very large kitchen. Some out-buildings formed a square with a large barn facing the house, in all about three acres.

"I'll mention it to Peg." He remembered the farm. They used to pick fruit there, filling strawberry punnits when he was younger.

After tea Ray mentioned the house to the others and all seemed interested. They decided to have a run out to have a look now the evenings were lighter. They piled into the car and set off. Along a long straight road Ray said "The turning's along here." Three miles further on, "I think we've passed it, I'm sure it's somewhere here." After turning the car around them retraced their steps at a slower pace. "There, it's there in those trees" they all shouted almost together. The opening was almost concealed by a line of trees. They drove down the lane and saw the house. At one time it would have been a splendid country farmhouse but now it looked a bit run down. Dr Bennet studied the house through a pair of binoculars he'd brought for the job.

"The roof looks sound and the brick work, it probably needs a bit of money spending on it and painting and decorating however it's got possibilities." Everyone had a look through the glasses. "Well, shall we give him a ring and make an appointment to view?"

Next weekend they visited the farmhouse, this time to view. The rooms were oak beamed with stone flagged floors and solid wooden floors in the bed rooms. The kitchen was large with an old - fashioned range and fire. The decor had been left too long and would have to be done again along with the bathroom, and a good central heating system installed. Not much in the way of building needed doing; it was just a case of bringing it up to modern standards. An oak stairway divided the house into two separate wings making it ideal. Pegs mum made her mind up. "I like it. Oh, it needs work but it has potential." Mr Jenkins on enquired if they had a property to sell, and when she said no and he saw the prospect of an immediate sale said: "I'll offer you a good reduction for a quick sale. I was going to put it into the agent's hands but if you're interested maybe we can do a deal."

The day ended with both party's exchanging solicitor's names. The house was sold subject to survey and contract. "Let's stop for a drink to celebrate." Mrs Mather was in a buoyant mood. A country inn a little way down the road looked inviting. It was very quiet this early evening. A waiter came for their orders as they sat down. The doctor had a scotch and soda, Pegs mum gin and tonic, Peg a lager, "and the boy," said the waiter looking at Ray who was eighteen but still looked fourteen. "He'll have half a lager too." The waiter looked but said nothing. A short time later he brought the drinks.

If we put two en-suite bathrooms in the two large bedrooms and then we; At this point Ray stopped listening, after all no-one asked his opinion or what he'd like, he was totally ignored as usual.

The day's passed quickly. Moving day came and they had to vacate their old property. The builders were in almost at once starting with the kitchen. Ray could now spend his time on the out side stripping and painting, his work as a shop fitter held him in good stead, and as the weeks passed and work progressed a transformation overtook the old place. The outside looked bright with new paintwork and pointing. Inside a large shiny new kitchen took shape and upstairs the en-suite bathrooms were installed. A nursery was made from one of the bedrooms as Peg was getting near her time.

August was the time of the wedding. "Ray," said Peg as they lay together in bed. "Mum wants' you to do her a favour. She wants' you to come to the wedding as a bridesmaid in your dress." "*What,* I can't do that. It would mean going out where everyone could see me." "They'll not know the difference when you get a little bit of make-up and do your hair. Do it to please mum." He went silent. How could they ask him to do such a thing, but how could he say no without hurting their feelings.

The day of the wedding Peg packed his dress into a suitcase in the morning. The ceremony was at one. "Come, let's get a tan." Peg now having given up work led him to the car driven by the doctor. Mrs Mather was in town picking up her wedding outfit. They arrived at the shop, it was deserted. All other appointments had been moved to the other shops. Peg selected a room in the solarium and undressed Ray. He lay on the table as he was creamed.

She aroused him slowly until he was moaning softly and then let him subside as she undressed and joined him on the sunbed, her swollen abdomen towering above him. Wrapped in towel's they went for a shower together.

"It's eleven and time for us to get ready." Peg took out a towelling robe from the suitcase and put it on Ray. One for herself was next. She took him by the hand into the shop. A knock sounded at the locked door, it was Mrs Mather. Peg let her in. "Did you get it," "Yes and it fit's perfectly, and I've got the ticket's so were all set."

Ray was seated in one of the salon chairs. Peg's mum took off her coat and set to work with the shampoo.

Ray's hair, which was already long because he'd been forbidden to have it cut, was now ideal for a new style. It was set in a feminine style by Peg's mum. When she had finished it looked completely different. He stared in the mirror at the unfamiliar image looking back at him. He started to rise out of the chair. Stay there he was told. A bag was produced, it contained make-up. His young face hardly needed foundation just a little blusher with lipstick and false eye-lashes, a touch of eye make-up and his eyebrows darkened and he was finished.

"Right, don't smudge it putting your dress on." Peg was speaking and leading him by the hand back upstairs. The robe was removed. "Foot," said Peg, holding the panties for him to step into. She was determined to dress him despite her figure. The stockings followed and then the suspender belt, and the padded bra. A slip was draped over his head to be followed by his mini-dress; the shoe's completed the job. Peg stood back and regarded her work. "You're beautiful, you really are, look." He looked in the full length mirror and didn't even recognise himself as this young girl looked back. Even he had to admit he/ she looked good.

The registry Office was crowded with guests from the previous marriage. Ray stood nervously holding the hem of his dress fully expecting someone to suddenly say: "It's a boy," and point at him. He hoped none of his old mates would put in an appearance. The office cleared, it was their turn. Ray stood behind as he couldn't be a witness and sign Raymond dressed as he was. A few of the doctor's friends came into the room. One of around nineteen stood next to Ray and started to chat. "Have you known the doctor long?" "About two years" answered Ray, hoping his voice wouldn't give him away. The young man didn't seem to notice anything was wrong with his voice and the wedding started. Being a witness he stood at the front, but his place was taken by two more of his friends who stood on either side of Ray, and each being over six foot tall dwarfed him.

The wedding was soon over; the young man had to leave immediately. He had a word with the couple before giving Ray a smile and he was gone. There was still the other two guests, and if they were doctors surely they could tell the difference between men and women, and then what would he say. "Excuse me, but I'm a bloke dressed in drag." The men spoke with the doctor and his bride shook his hand and kissed her on the cheek, said goodbye to Peg and kissed her and came to Ray. This is it. He thought, the man took his hand said goodbye and kissed *him*, to be followed by the second man. He'd not been found out. The foursome went for a drink before the newly weds went to the airport, this time his drink was brought without any question of his age.

Now Peg's mum turned to him. "I'm glad you put on your dress for me, your far more beautiful than Peg ever was, I'll bring you back another one as a present." Peg smiled at the remark about him being better looking, but sadly it was true. She was big boned and never slim, more of a tom boy. Ray wanted to say "I don't want another dress," but thought it may sound ungrateful, he therefore said nothing.

Time to go, the drinks were finished and as they were walking to the door the Dr said he'd better go to the loo before driving. Ray also decided to go and followed the doctor. Moments later he suddenly realised he was in the gents lavatory dressed as a girl. He dashed out and made his way to the ladies hoping no-one had seen.

They were dropped at home and the newlyweds went to the airport to catch their flight. "I'll get changed," said Ray making for the stairs. Peg took him by the wrist. "No, I like to see you in your dress," she kissed him. "There I've smudged your lipstick." Peg wiped the offending smudge with her handkerchief, "We'll have an early tea, and will you help." They made a meal between them Ray having been provided with an apron and settled down for the evening.

Two weeks later the Dr and now Mrs Bennet returned just in time as Peg started with the baby. They had a son. Ray took flowers feeling proud just as any new father. He said mum would visit later that day.

The following week they were in the kitchen of the farm-house discussing names for the baby. At last they chose Robin. "By the way you haven't opened your present yet," said Peg's mum, "I'm sure Peg would like to see it." Ray was hoping it would be forgotten. "No, I haven't had time; I've been busy decorating the nursery." "Well bring it down and open it, I'm dying to see it myself," urged Peg.

Ray reluctantly made his way upstairs to fetch the box. He carried it down and laid it on the table. It was tied with a large pink bow with a card addressed to the most beautiful girl in the world. He read and winced, his fingers slowly easing the lid off. Tissue paper was pulled back to reveal a black dress. He lifted it out of the box. It resembled a cocktail dress with skirt and a fitted bodice but was strapless. Peg squealed, "Oh, it's lovely, but how will he keep it up?" "You'll see," said mum. Under the dress was a pair of black shoes and under the shoes frilly lace of black underwear showed. Ray lifted it out of the box. It was a Basque set with black stockings. His heart sank. He knew what was coming next. Peg took his hand, "Come love, let's go and try it on." He allowed himself to be led up to their bedroom and stood still as Peg undressed him. Once again he watched as the transformation took place, as he became her. Everything fitted perfectly. It was strange to have bare shoulders when dressed; all he needed was a cleavage. Instead Peg hung a necklace around his neck finished off with diamond earrings, a touch of make-up and he was ready.

They went downstairs together. Peg rushed into the kitchen. "Close your eye's you two, are they closed, Right, presenting Miss World here before your very eyes." She faked a drum roll. "Now, open them." Ray braced himself, he knew what was coming next, how beautiful how it fitted, it had all been said before.

He waited, nothing, just silence. They just sat there looking at him. "Well," it was Peg impatient as ever. Her mum finally spoke. "I'm lost for words. I never thought anyone could look so great, he's stunning." The Doctor nodded in agreement. Peg smiled in triumph. "He is though isn't he" Ray had to parade up and down the kitchen. "That's too good to wear in the house; it'll have to be saved for best. Pity about the cleavage or he could wear it out."

Ray had to wear the dress for the rest of the evening and was thankful when it was time for bed.

Peg returned to work a few weeks later leaving Ray to cope with the baby. The builders had finally finished the house and barn and had just one of the outhouses left. Ray had the place to him alone and spent his time cleaning and learning to cook simple meals for the returning workers. They would select the menu and tell him how to cook the meal and leave him to it. After a time he began to make simple but passable meals.

In November he found a job. It didn't pay a lot but it was a start. Trouble was if he started working who would look after the baby and do the evening meal. They would have to get someone in or Peg would have to stop work. Either way nothing would be gained financially or a lot would be lost in convenience. He was persuaded not to take it.

Christmas came; his present included a make-up kit and another dress. He now had three dresses, underwear and shoes.

The builders had gone, their work completed. Now he was at home alone all day with the baby. He learning to do the washing and ironing when he noticed his boxer shorts were missing. When Peg came home he asked about them. They had a hole in she replied and had been throw away along with two old pairs of jeans.

Now and then he had to dress up for them at the weekend but apart from that everything seemed all right. He was at last persuaded to sign off at the Job Centre and make the housework his full time work.

The only time he got to town was when they went shopping in the car. The house being isolated didn't get any callers.

They're nineteenth birthday's were coming up. As the shop was busy it was decided to have a holiday at the seaside a little later in April when it was still quiet. During the evening meal Mrs Bennet said, "Why not go as two girls, it will be good practice." "That's a great idea," Peg was all for it, giving Ray's hand a squeeze. "I don't want to go as a girl." Protested Ray, but the ladies as usual were not listening to him. "He'll need more dresses, let's go to the car boot sale in the morning, there's bound to be some.

Ray was left alone in the morning to look after his son whilst the women went to the sale. He knew it was no use in arguing with them once their minds were made up. He got on with the household tasks that had become his.

Just before lunch the car returned to the house. Peg entered carrying some dresses. She was followed by her mother with a bag of shoes and handbags also three skirts draped over her arm. Peg advanced into the kitchen. "We've had a good day with lots of great things for you, look!" and held up a skirt. "Just slip into this," she said as she was already unbuckling his belt. Ray did as he was told and stepped into the skirt allowing his jeans to be pulled down and then off. The skirt was zipped and a pair of shoes put onto his feet. The women stood back to regard him. "Hmm, yes, I think tights with that, something medium like American Tan." Ray had to stay in the skirt the rest of the day. The women were in a world of their own planning what he was going to wear.

Just before the start of the holiday Mrs Bennet became ill and couldn't work. Peg stepped in to run the business and the holiday was postponed until May. Nothing more was said about the holiday until mid April when Mrs Bennet had recovered to run the business once more. Peg announced she had re-booked now every evening Peg wanted to dress him trying all the different combinations of clothes and shoes.

One week before the holiday Peg handed him a dress. "Wear this today." Ray, dressed in his jeans, suddenly rebelled. "No I won't. I've had enough of dresses. I'm not wearing any more." He picked up the skirt and tore the skirt up to the waistband and threw it down. Peg picked up the torn garment and examined the tear, then took hold of his wrist and dragged him down to the kitchen where her mother and the doctor were having breakfast.

"Just look at what he's done, it's ruined. And he says he won't dress again, well, we'll see about that," "Mum" Pegs mum rose from the table, and took his other wrist and he was dragged to the door. Ray didn't like this and dug his heels in refusing to be moved. The next moment he was picking himself up from the floor. With one blow Peg had knocked him to the ground. He was shocked. His wife had hit him.

They dragged him outside still in a daze. The barn across the courtyard had its doors open. Once inside a rope was lashed around his wrists and hooked onto a pulley. This was pulled up tight until his toes were just touching the ground and he was at full stretch.

Peg disappeared from the barn returning moments later with the kitchen scissors. Ray saw the angry expression on her face as she neared. His T-shirt was grabbed, the scissors were put at the bottom and then it was cut up the front and across each sleeve. It fell away just a rag. His vest was next for the same treatment. Peg took hold of his belt and instead of unbuckling cut it in half. The waistband presented no problem. His jeans were cut down each leg until they fell to the ground. His shoes were next then the socks cut away leaving him in just his last pair of boxer shorts. The scissors approached, he kicked out. Peg's mum grabbed his legs. Peg took hold of the shorts, two snips and he was naked with all his clothes in rags at his feet. He was naked in front of his mother - in law.

"Now we'll see what you will or won't wear," Peg picked up the cut belt and walked behind him. He guessed what was about to happen and pleaded, "don't please don't" It fell on deaf ears as the strap fell on his bare buttocks. Again and again then up his back until he was screaming with pain. The rope slackened, he fell in a heap onto the earthen floor. The women took hold of the rope on his wrists and pulled him to the side of the barn where he was dumped onto a pile of straw. The doors were closed leaving him naked, and sobbing quietly on the straw.

It was evening before the doors opened again. Mrs Bennet entered carrying a bowl of soup. It was placed before him and she left, closing the doors again. He was alone in the darkness. The soup was hot. I may as well eat it as it doesn't look as though there's anything else to night.

In the morning Peg brought him some cereal for breakfast. "Let me come in he pleaded." "You know what you have to do." "No!" Ray showed defiance again Peg picked up the strap. "Stand up and bend over." "No" Ray was still defiant. "If you don't you'll get it worse, now do as I say." Ray knew he was beaten. He slowly got to his feet and bent over. He watched as Peg moved to his rear. A stinging blow with the strap fell on his sore behind to be followed by another. Tears sprang to his eyes once more. "Now eat your cereal." She closed the doors.

It was a cold night. Ray tried to bury beneath the straw to keep warm, but even with the straw he shivered for most of the time. There hadn't been anything to eat but the one bowl of cereal all day. No one came at night. Now he awaited the door's opening.

Daylight showed through the crack's at the door's edge. It finally opened. Peg entered with food, and placed it in front of him as Ray crawled from beneath the straw. "Well," she asked. "Please Peg," he cried. Peg marched out leaving him alone again. He ate his breakfast at least there was a mug of hot tea.

That evening Mrs Bennet came with a plate of hot stew. "Where are you?" Ray lifted his head from the straw. "Come out." Ray didn't move he was too embarrassed being totally naked. "If you don't get up I'm taking the stew away." By now he was so hungry he crawled out. "Stand up," she ordered. He stood trying to cover himself with his hands.

"Put them behind your back, we all know what you've got. He did so leaving himself exposed. "You've got to stop this silliness. You look very pretty as a girl, far better than as a boy. Now, are you going to dress for me?" Ray thought about it. It was obvious he wasn't going to win, he therefore nodded his head. "That's better, but you must want to rather than be made to, we'll see in the morning." She picked up the dirty dishes and walked out closing the doors behind her.

Peg came next morning. Ray after another cold night in the straw begged her to release him. He crawled out of the straw on his hands and knees sobbing. "Please let me come home, I'll do anything you say. I want to dress for you to make you happy, please let me." Peg stooped down and ran her hand over his naked shoulders. She kissed him tenderly. "Hush pet," she said. "Why did you make us so angry, we love you? Now let's have no more of this nonsense, you can come in and apologise to everyone and it'll be alright."

Peg helped him to his feet. They walked back to the farmhouse and entered the kitchen. The Doctor and Mrs Bennet were there. Ray fell to his knees sobbing and asking their forgiveness. The Dr took a small case from his inside pocket. It contained a small bottle and a hypodermic needle. He filled the hypodermic from the bottle and injected Ray. "Go and get a bath, you're dirty. Peg pulled him to his feet and pushed him still naked towards the stairs.

He ran a hot bath and lay in the water letting the warmth seep into his bones. After bathing he dried himself and put on a bath robe. Peg was waiting for him in the bedroom. She handed him a pair of panties and the padded bra. This time he put them on without a murmur. A red mini-skirt was on the bed together with a white blouse. Peg handed them to him. A pair of white ankle socks and his trainers finished the dressing. Peg sat him down and applied a touch of make-up and brushed his hair. "Now you look pretty again," giving him a kiss. She then walked over to the clothes closet. "Let's have a look at what you've got here and threw the doors wide open. She took out his suit and jeans and threw them onto the bed. "Take those downstairs and come back." Ray gathered the clothes and made his way downstairs depositing them on the kitchen table. On his return the bed was full with his shirts and socks, also his coat and shoes and the last of his underwear. These were taken down to be added to the pile on the table.

Peg came into the kitchen. "Go and burn those rags in the barn." Ray went to the barn and collected the rags with a pile of straw and filled a large metal skip they used for burning rubbish. The straw quickly caught and flared up. He added some pieces of wood and soon a fierce blaze was going. He put the rags on the fire and watched as they burned.

The car with Mrs Bennet arrived; she must have gone out while Ray was in the bath. Peg went over and began talking to her. They both disappeared into the house and returned with Ray's clothes. Peg began talking: "It's too upsetting to be changing from boy to girl so we've decided you don't have to any more." For a moment Ray couldn't believe it until peg handed him his clothes and said, "Here, burn them, you won't need them any more." They were right, he wouldn't have to change from boy to girl, and he would be a girl all the time. Ray held on to his suit until he saw the look in their eyes and realised if he defied them he would be back in the barn. He threw the suit onto the flames to be followed by the rest of his clothes. The only garments left were all female, now he'd no choice but to dress up everyday.

"Were going to work and I've left you a note of what to get for this evening." Ray watched the car pull away with the baby in the car seat. He was once again alone in the house. Once again tears sprang to his eyes as he dashed upstairs and took a hold-all from the closet to pack some things.

It was only after he'd packed some spare panties and a skirt and extra dress that he realised how ridiculous it was that a nineteen year old man was packing skirts and panties for himself. Still it was no more ridiculous than leaving in a mini-skirt. He picked up the bag and left walking down the road. After ten minutes he stopped. Where was he going? It suddenly dawned on him he'd no-where to go. No friends or money. A feeling of loneliness came over him and tears filled his eyes. Crying all the time had to stop, he told himself as he turned around and headed for the only world he knew.

Weekend saw them heading for the seaside and their holiday. The baby had been left at home. Arriving at the small hotel Peg signed for the two of them, only just remembering to put Ray's initial and not name. Shown to their room, to the hotel they were two girls together but Ray would have to have a change of name or give the game away. Keeping to the same initial Ray became Rita.

The first full day being a Sunday they went for a walk before lunch. The day was fine and sunny although not too hot for this time of year, but warm enough not to need a coat during the day. Peg had chosen a blue mini-dress with shoulder bag for Rita and for herself a mauve trouser-suit. When they returned to the hotel and lunch they were shown their table in the dining room. Next to them were two young men of about twenty. Soon they were glancing across at the two young ladies. Rita being sideways on to the young men hadn't noticed but Peg had, she smiled at them. Later as they sat in the lounge the young men approached and began a conversation. Rita was now aware of how short the dress was. When walking it was fine, but sitting down the skirt rode too far up the leg and he was afraid of showing too much. He self consciously tugged the hem down as much as possible, but was only drawing attention to himself and his legs. The young man took his hand and remarked on how tiny it was and noticed the fresh painted nails nicely manicured by Peg. The rings had been left at the farm house.

The boys were leaving in the morning and would the girls like to go to a disco with them on their last night? Rita was just about to refuse when he heard Peg saying they'd love to. That afternoon all four stayed together sightseeing. The boys split them into couples. Their names were Bob and Jack. Bob took Rita's hand around his back and put his arm around Rita's waist as they were walking. Peg was watching and could tell the boys were completely taken in by Rita. After the evening meal they retired to change for the disco. Rita was given the white mini-dress to wear. Peg changed into a blue dress, the only one she had. Rita thought this was only the second time he'd seen her in a dress.

Peg brushed his hair and applied his make-up, put on false eyelashes with a touch of mascara, when complete Peg stood back to look at her handiwork. "You'll do." Rita knew this meant he looked good. They descended the stairs where the boy's were waiting for them. Bob took one look. "Wow, you look great." and gave Rita a kiss. Before Rita had time to react he was being led out of the hotel and onto the street.

The disco was as usual, loud with flashing lights. The floor was crowded and the bar packed, in fact just as normal, an ordinary place. Rita was passable at disco dancing as they used to dance in the children's home. Peg too was good. Bob gave Rita his full attendance. Peg could see he was taken with her.

After the dance they walked home, or to the hotel. The boys would be gone tomorrow. "Why weren't you here last week, we could have had a great time."

In the lounge a coffee percolator was placed for guests to help themselves. They made coffee and sat down, at least Peg and Jack did. Bob sat in a chair as Jack placed the coffee cup on a table besides him. He took Rita's wrist and pulled *her* onto his knee. The mini- skirt rode up onto the thigh and Bobs hand automatically held *her* leg to stop *her* falling off.

Rita could feel him stroking *her* thigh, the fingers going under the skirt nearly up to the white panties. Bob leaned back into the chair bringing Rita onto his chest. He kissed *her* on the lips. Rita could not help but respond although he knew he shouldn't. Bob was getting very passionate, his hand shifted to the inner thigh, stroking and going higher each time. Rita responded with more ardent kisses but knew it had to stop before the truth came out. *She* pulled away. "What's wrong?" asked Bob. "I've got a boy friend back home that I love, it wouldn't be right for us." Bob was crestfallen. "Oh, I see, sorry, I thought, well," he just couldn't find the words. Rita came to his rescue. *She* gave Bob a kiss. "I like you a lot, if things were different." Another kiss and Rita said goodnight.

Peg followed shortly afterwards. She was beaming. "You really turned him on." "Yes," said Rita a little sadly. "I wish I hadn't, I liked him a lot. The thing is Peg I enjoyed kissing him as much as he enjoyed me." Peg said nothing, but smiled.

Next morning came more goodbyes. They exchanged numbers and promised to call although they both knew they wouldn't. A last kiss and the boy's were gone. The rest of the week passed quietly. A couple of shows were opening and a few drinks in the local bars passed the time, but after the boy's had gone everything seemed a little flat. On arriving home Peg could hardly wait to tell of the encounter with the boy's, recounting in detail Rita's passionate embraces with Bob. Dr Bennet was there with his needle to continue the injections. Rita wondered about them as he felt great. He recommended looking after the baby just as before. That evening in their bedroom Peg told him how proud she was of him at the disco, and how lovely he looked. She undressed him until he was naked. "Let's not bother with the nightie tonight love."

The morning saw Peg take Rita to town to have his ear's pierced and gold sleepers put in, then on to the shop to have his hair done. He left the shop pushing the baby in a push chair. No matter how he tried he couldn't forget Bob. Why had Peg let him go so far without saying anything or stopping him or doing something but she just sat there watching. His mind was in a whirl as he walked along listening to the click clack of his high heels echoing along the pavement. He reached town. The first stop was to the jewellers to pick up a watch being repaired for Mrs Bennet. His next call was to the dry cleaners, further into the centre. The traffic was busy but the road was separated by railings from the pavement. He spotted someone familiar walking towards him. With a start he recognised it was his old workmate and former school-mate who'd known him for years. Rita looked for a way out. The railings blocked one route and no convenient shop door-way offered an escape. Short of turning around he was stuck. His steps faltered as he hesitated and deciding it was too late, pressed on trying not to look at the approaching figure. At any moment he expected a familiar voice to say, "Hello, Ratty what's the fancy dress for?" Rita walked on, any moment now. He passed bye, he walked past and didn't recognise me. Rita had a quick glance back. His old mate was still walking away and had walked on without a backward glance. Rita's nervous habit of fingering the hem of his mini-skirt becoming all too obvious as she watched there was no doubt she'd got away with it. A smile came across his face. If his former friend didn't know him then maybe nobody would. He continued walking down the street the click clack of his heels going a little faster now.

It was a new experience for him and now for the first time he really enjoyed being a girl. He stopped at a shop window pretending to look in at the goods on display but in reality was studying his own reflection in the glass. A very pretty petite girl stared back at him. He looked at his legs in their tights, very passable, the little skirt suited his figure, and with his hair now in a feminine style he realised it was true, he did make a better girl than a boy and for the first time he was actually pleased.

That evening he waited as the car drew up at the farmhouse. Peg came into the kitchen first. Rita put his arms around her neck and gave a great big kiss. "Well, thank you, but what's this all about?" Rita told her of the encounter with his school mate. "That's the first time I wanted to be a girl. I'm glad you made me wear dresses and I do look better." He kissed her again. Peg was overcome with emotion. "Oh pet," was all she could say as she kissed him back.

What's all this then, Mrs Bennet said as she came in to the kitchen and found the two of them in an embrace. Rita repeated the words he'd spoken to Peg. Mrs Bennet gave him a hug with tear's in her eyes. "I'm so pleased for you, now you better have a word with the doctor." Dr Bennet entered the kitchen to find three women waiting for him and looking at him in an expectant way. "What?" he asked. "Rita wants a word with you as he's decided to become a real girl." Peg blurted out before Rita could say anything. "Are you sure it's what you want?" asked the doctor. Rita nodded. "We'll talk about it this evening."

They sat around the table after the evening meal. The doctor spoke: "Are you sure you want to be a girl rather than a boy?" "Yes I'm certain." Rita replied. "And you Peg, are you sure." Peg nodded. "Then you better tell Rita." Peg turned and took his hand. "You want to become a girl. I want to become a boy." A curtain seemed to have been lifted from Rita's eyes. It all made sense now. Peg not wearing dresses but yet wanting him to. The fascination she had of his body in particular his genitals, and why Peg always took the lead in love making. When they saw Ray at the shop he fitted the bill perfectly. No parents or relatives, no friends or home, a petite figure that would look right in a dress and yet man enough to give Peg a child before any sex change. He would make an ideal wife to Peg's husband. Peg took his hand. "The first time I saw you looking like a little boy lost, I fell in love with you, and I love you more now." "Soppy," said Rita.

One week later they were in a small hotel on the continent. The doctor had arranged an interview with a consultant at a private clinic. Ray's passport had not been altered and he still looked boyish although wearing female clothing. Customs were too busy to check too closely or enquire as to why, or maybe they were used to seeing male / female dress and passed them through. After checking into the clinic they retired to their room. Peg started to undress Rita. She took off the padded bra, "look," she said, and pointed to Rita's breasts. The nipples now stood out in little points. Now Rita knew what the injections were for. They were hormone's to make his breast grow.

"Dr Haas will see you now." The nurse showed them in to the office. The Dr told them of the operations each of them would have but it would be a while before he could fit them in, in the meantime they would have counselling. These courses were to assess the state of mind of the people who wished to change gender. Stage one was over.

The months passed and they were given a date for the operations. Peg would have two operations. The first one to remove her breasts would be at the same time as Rita's sex change, followed three months later by her Peg's sex change. The padding had now been done away with as Rita had a bust in her own right and implants had done the rest. "Let's go out to celebrate," said the doctor.

The club was one of the best in the district, serving only the best food and finest wines. Peg took Rita's hand. "Will you wear your black dress for me?" "Oh yes," echoed Mrs Bennet. Rita went upstairs to the bedroom. The dress had been put away for a special occasion. He took out the box and opened it laying the dress and underwear on the bed whilst he had a shower, then dressed. This time the bodice fitted his bust showing just enough cleavage. He finished with the shoes and diamond earrings and with a touch of perfume made his way down.

The three were waiting for him as he entered the kitchen. They gazed upon him without saying a word. "Wow," the doctor finally said. Peg took his hand. "You look stunning," she said kissing him softly. "Now wait here for the baby sitter whilst we get changed. The table's booked for eight so we've plenty of time."

The Country Club dinner dance was crowded with all available tables booked. After the meal there was general dancing on the small floor. Rita could disco but not do modern dancing but soon it didn't matter as there was no room to do anything but disco. He made a mental note to learn in future. The conversation turned to the forthcoming operations. Once Peg had her mastectomy she could start with hormone treatment and pass as a man.

The dinner was good and the wine flowed until all felt the warm glow inside. The band played until the early hours when people began leaving. The doctor had arranged for a taxi to take them home and at two am they collected their coats and made their way outside. The taxi was waiting for them. The driver got out of the cab and opened the door. The doctor and Mrs Bennet got in to be followed by Peg and as Rita was about to board he felt his hand being taken. A voice said, "Rita is that you?" He looked, it was Bob. "Rita I tried to phone but couldn't get through, how are you, you look lovely, is that Peg with you?" Rita became aware of the others watching from the cab. "Peg, it's Bob, he's our driver." "In that case hadn't we better be going?" It was the doctor from the cab. "Oh yes, I forgot." said Bob as he ushered Rita into the cab and walked to the driver's door.

Arriving at the farmhouse Peg engaged Bob in a long conversation as the others alighted. In the kitchen they waited for Peg as the sound of the taxi was heard driving away. "You've been ages, what were you talking about?" Mum asked impatiently. "Just about the holiday we'd had. He said that he'd have liked it to be longer."

The date for the operations arrived. They said there farewells and boarded the ferry for the continent. This time they booked straight into the clinic where they were in adjacent rooms. After tests Rita operation was scheduled for two in the afternoon, and Pegs later in the day. She stayed with Rita until it was time and the porter came for him. One last kiss and he was gone.

Rita awoke the next morning with a dry mouth and a dull ache in the groin. He felt the bandages but now there was no bulge, now he was a girl. A nurse approached. "How are you young lady?" Rita smiled, at least in appearances he was a young lady. "I'm fine; do you know how Peg is?"

A week later they were well enough to leave the clinic and catch the ferry home.

Mrs Bennet welcomed them with open arms. "We shall have to think of a new name for you young lady or do you want to be Rita?" Peg interrupted. "We've decided to simply exchange names. I will become Ray and Ray will become Peg. This way we won't have any difficulty with birth certificates and the baby need never know. Also our marriage will still be valid as we will be man and wife. "That's a great idea, have they given you a final date for your second operation?" "Yes said Peg in three months when Ray goes for his check-up. Dr Bennet arrived home with a bottle of champagne. "For the young lady," he said, presenting it to Ray. We'd better open it and drink to our new daughter and her husband.

Peg now gave up work. Her voice was becoming a little huskier and the first sign of hair had started growing on her face as the hormones took effect. A new wardrobe was bought ready for after her operation and her new life. Ray looked after his son and in the meantime took dancing lessons. They exchanged jewellery, not that Ray had anything of value except his ring and as he had smaller hands would be keeping it.

The weeks passed and the time had come for the operation. Ray was to book into a small hotel besides the clinic and stay there until Pegs operation was over. After Peg had recovered they planned to exchange names and return as man and wife.

The day of the operation they found Peg had been allocated the same room as Ray had used. The same doctor was looking after them, also the same nurse who greeted them as old friends.

Tests were carried out in the morning and the doctor talked through the op with Peg promising there wouldn't be any scars showing afterwards. In the afternoon after the pre -med Ray had to leave for his check-up. He went to another room to have his examination. He undressed and put on a robe. The doctor entered with the nurse. "Disrobe please and lie on the couch. Ray did so and for the first time felt slightly embarrassed at showing his female form for the first time. Afterwards the doctor told him he could have normal sexual relation as a woman although still having to take hormones. Pegs op took place later that day. Ray visited the clinic but Peg was still asleep. The nurse said everything was as it should be and Peg would sleep until morning.

Ray went back to the hotel and ordered a meal in the dining room. As he sat at the table a pair of hands covered his eyes and a voice said: "Guess who?" He knew at once from the voice. "It's Bob" "Oh, you guessed." Bob sat down at the table. "I heard you lost your husband. Peg rang me and told me you'd be here tonight visiting. It seems a shame to be alone like this, let's make a night of it. What do you say Rita," using the name he'd known Ray as the first time they met. Ray knew Peg had arranged the meeting therefore It must be alright.

They ate in the hotel. Bob was good company and Ray soon forgot the arranged meeting. "Shall we go to the disco, it's just down the street," Bob suggested. Ray agreed. "I'll have to change first, give me ten minutes." and left to go up to his room. On the pillow was a letter from Peg. It read; Just in case my op doesn't go too well I'd like you to be with a man at least once.

Do it for me! Love Peg.

Ray got back downstairs to Bob. "Is anything wrong." he asked. "No, nothing," said Ray, "come on let's go".

They stopped at the disco until late and then made their way back to the hotel. Bob told Ray he had to see him one more time as he was leaving to live abroad. They entered the lift to go to their rooms on the same floor. The doors closed and the lift started its ascent. Bob took Ray in his arms and kissed him gently. Ray found himself responding though he didn't mean to. The doors opened they walked to Ray's room and he unlocked the door. Turning to say goodnight to Bob he found himself in a passionate embrace once again. No, he was going to say, but the words were stifled by kisses. Once again he responded, and then felt the zip of his dress being lowered. He tried to push Bob away but the dress fell to the floor. A voice inside told him it wasn't right and therefore he kept on resisting. The bra strap was unhooked and Bob's hand came round the side and pushed the bra up revealing Ray's new breasts. His hand cupped the breast and the fingers tease the nipple as Ray felt himself lifted and carried to the bed. He now responded pulling Bob's shirt up and caressing his back until the shirt was thrown off along with the pants. A hand crept down to the panties Ray was wearing and pushed them down. Ray gasped as he felt Bob enter him. The doctor said he could have normal sexual relations but he never believed him until now.

Later Bob ran a bath and they bathed together drinking wine from a bottle. The next day Bob was gone forever, leaving a fond memory neither would forget.

Ray walked alone to the clinic. Peg was sitting up in Bed. As soon as Ray entered she asked, "How did you get on, did you see Bob and did you behave yourself," she added with a mischievous grin. Ray told her about the night before. "Good, I'm glad. I wanted you to have the experience at least once just in case." Ray reached into the handbag and gave Peg a present. Peg opened the box and took out a gents gold wrist watch. "Read what it say's," he said. Peg read. To my darling husband Ray with all my love, Peg. This is for you. It's now you name, Raymond, and from today I'll become Margaret, but you can call me Peg, and then ducked as *Ray* took a swipe at *her*.

Three months later and a holiday booked in the sun. *Peg* had packed making sure the mini trunks were included. *She* was determined to get *her* own back for the first holiday but before then a wedding. They were being married in a full church ceremony, or having a blessing as they were already wed. All their friends would be there at the formal occasion. Dr Bennet was giving the bride away and one of his colleague's was to be best man. Their son was a page. Afterwards a reception was to be held and photographs taken.

Peg now Ray, was in morning dress and Ray now Peg looked radiant in her bridle gown as *she* entered the church. Now they could both feel as though they were married. *Peg* saw *Ray* waiting at the Altar as *she* walked down the nave of the church. A tear of happiness rolled down *her* cheek. 'Hope that doesn't spoil my make-up' *she* thought.

Laying on the sun-bed at their holiday hotel, *Peg* asked *Ray*, "Do you remember the white mini-dress you bought on our honeymoon," and went on, "Who did you buy it for?" *Ray* smiled, "It was bought for you, we wondered if you'd notice it was far too small for me. Mum and I planned it. I told her to give me fifteen minutes and then come upstairs to see you in the dress. We were going to gradually dress you but when you rebelled you upset our plans, but then we realised we could turn it to our advantage by getting rid of all your clothes at once. I wish I'd included these trunks though." *Ray* was wearing the mini trunks that *Peg* had insisted he wore. *Peg* put some cream onto *Ray's* manly chest and rubbed it in going down to the trunks. She ran her fingers lightly over the bulge. "They are a bit cheeky aren't they?" *Ray* had to laugh; after all, *he'd* bought them. They laid on the beds side by side holding hands. "Tonight I'm going to do the undressing" she said. *He* gave her hand a squeeze.